D1278675

# Book 2

# Miss Annie
# ROOFTOP
# CAT

Frank Le Gall
Illustrated by Flore Balthazar
Coloring by Robin Doo

Graphic Universe™ • Minneapolis • New York

Zeno's philosophical quote to Miss Annie on page 25 is part of Krishna's
advice to Arjuna in the sacred Hindu book the *Bhagavad Gita*,
which is part of the ancient Indian epic the *Mahabharata*.

Story by Frank Le Gall
Art by Flore Balthazar
Coloring by Robin Doo

Translation by Carol Klio Burrell

English translation copyright © 2012 by Lerner Publishing Group, Inc.

First American edition published in 2012 by Graphic Universe™. Published by arrangement with
MEDIATOON LICENSING – France.

Miss Annie
© DUPUIS 2010 – Balthazar & Le Gall
www.dupuis.com

Graphic Universe™ is a trademark of Lerner Publishing Group, Inc.

Graphic Universe™
A division of Lerner Publishing Group, Inc.
241 First Avenue North
Minneapolis, MN 55401 U.S.A.

Website address: www.lernerbooks.com


Library of Congress Cataloging-in-Publication Data

Le Gall, Frank, 1959–
       Rooftop cat / by Frank Le Gall ; illustrated by Flore Balthazar.
       p.    cm. – (Miss Annie ; #2)
       Summary: Miss Annie, a young kitten, joins a group of cats in her neighborhood and, through
    their rivalry with other groups, learns about loyalty, courage, and the dangers of the world she is
    so eager to explore, helping her best mouse friend to become braver along the way.
       ISBN: 978-0-7613-7885-3 (lib. bdg. : alk. paper)
       1. Graphic novels. [1. Graphic novels. 2. Cats—Fiction. 3. Animals—Infancy—Fiction. 4. Mice—
    Fiction.] I. Balthazar, Flore, ill. II. Title.
    PZ7.7.L42Roo 2012
    741.5′973–dc23                                                          2011025646

Manufactured in the United States of America
1 – DP – 12/31/11

# I. At Night, All Cats Are Gray

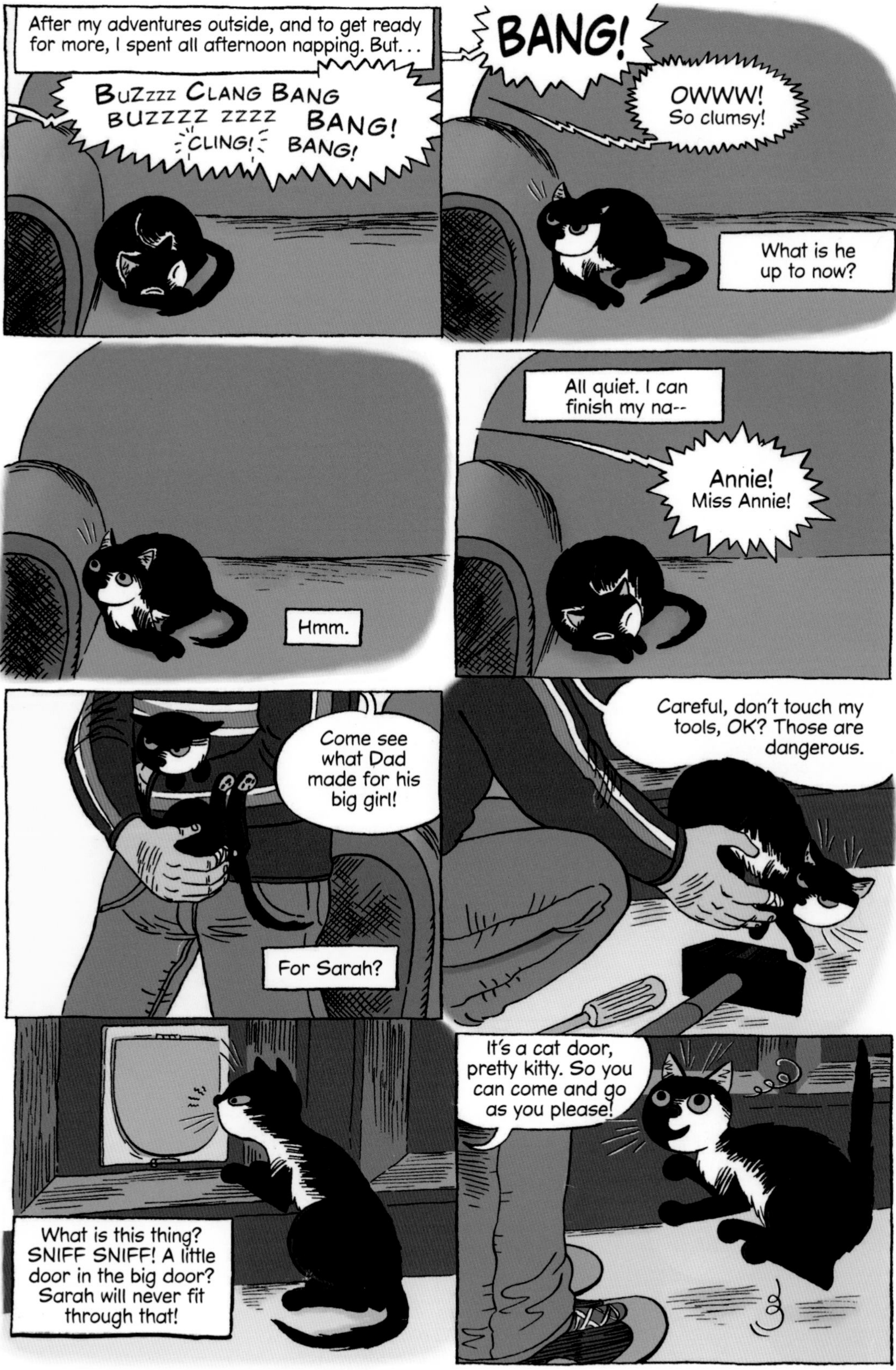
After my adventures outside, and to get ready for more, I spent all afternoon napping. But. . .
BuZzzz Clang Bang
BUZZZZ zzzz
CLING!
BANG!
BANG!
BANG!
OWWW! So clumsy!
What is he up to now?
Hmm.
All quiet. I can finish my na--
Annie! Miss Annie!
Come see what Dad made for his big girl!
For Sarah?
Careful, don't touch my tools, OK? Those are dangerous.
What is this thing? SNIFF SNIFF! A little door in the big door? Sarah will never fit through that!
It's a cat door, pretty kitty. So you can come and go as you please!

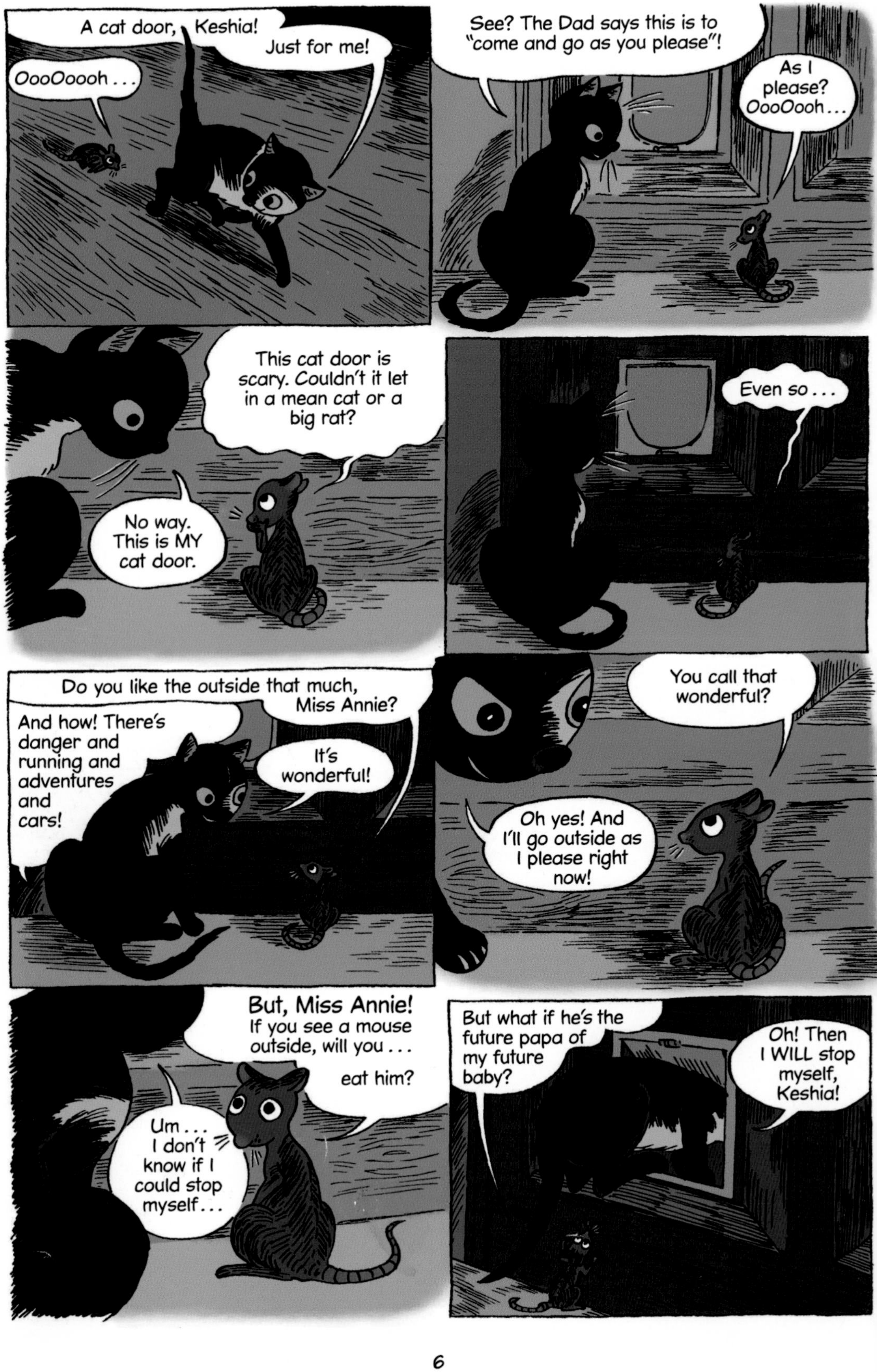
A cat door, Keshia!
Just for me!
OooOoooh . . .
See? The Dad says this is to "come and go as you please"!
As I please? OooOooh . . .
This cat door is scary. Couldn't it let in a mean cat or a big rat?
No way. This is MY cat door.
Even so . . .
Do you like the outside that much, Miss Annie?
And how! There's danger and running and adventures and cars!
It's wonderful!
You call that wonderful?
Oh yes! And I'll go outside as I please right now!
But, Miss Annie! If you see a mouse outside, will you . . .
eat him?
Um . . . I don't know if I could stop myself . . .
But what if he's the future papa of my future baby?
Oh! Then I WILL stop myself, Keshia!

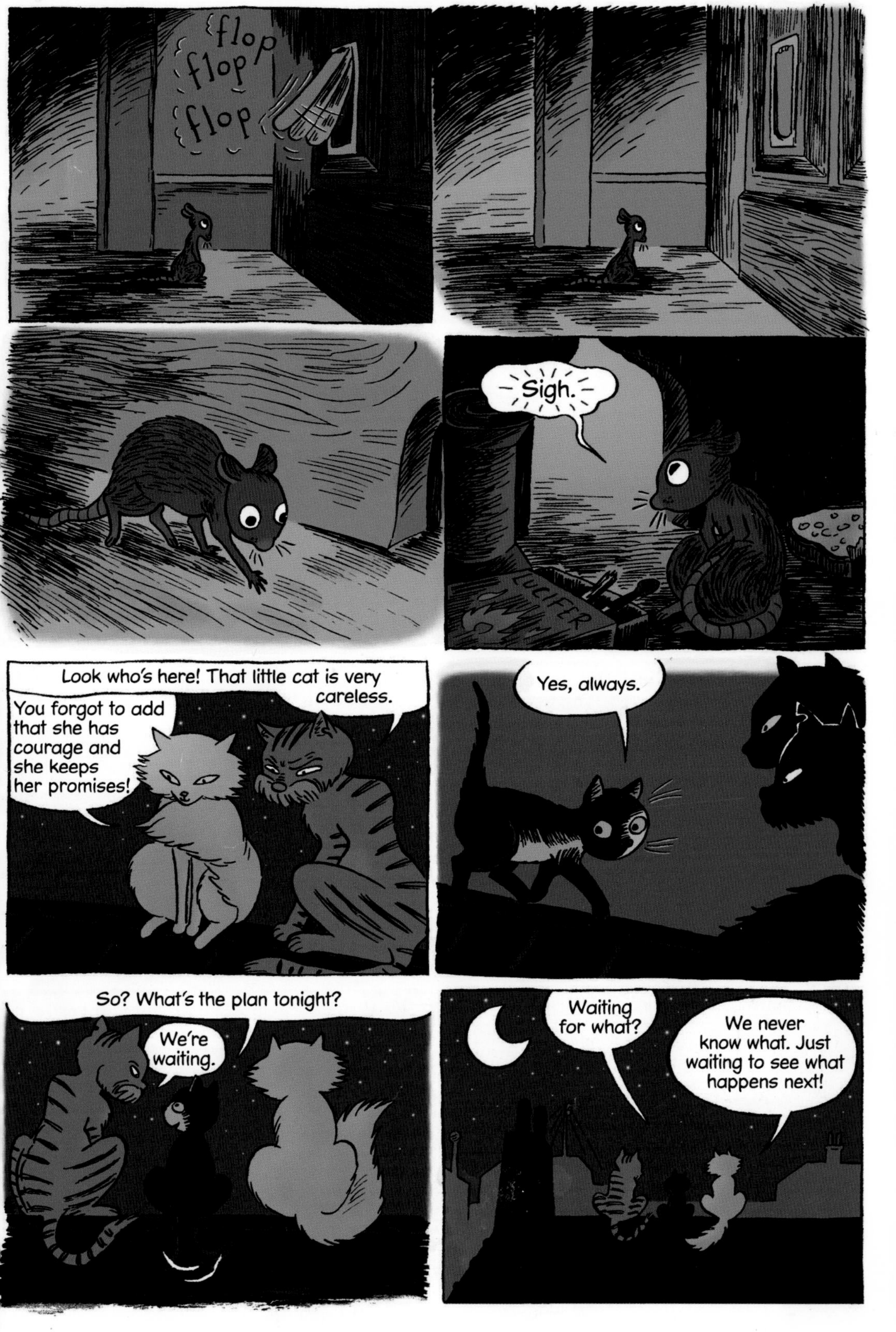
flop
flop
flop
Sigh.
LUCIFER
Look who's here! That little cat is very careless.
You forgot to add that she has courage and she keeps her promises!
Yes, always.
So? What's the plan tonight?
We're waiting.
Waiting for what?
We never know what. Just waiting to see what happens next!

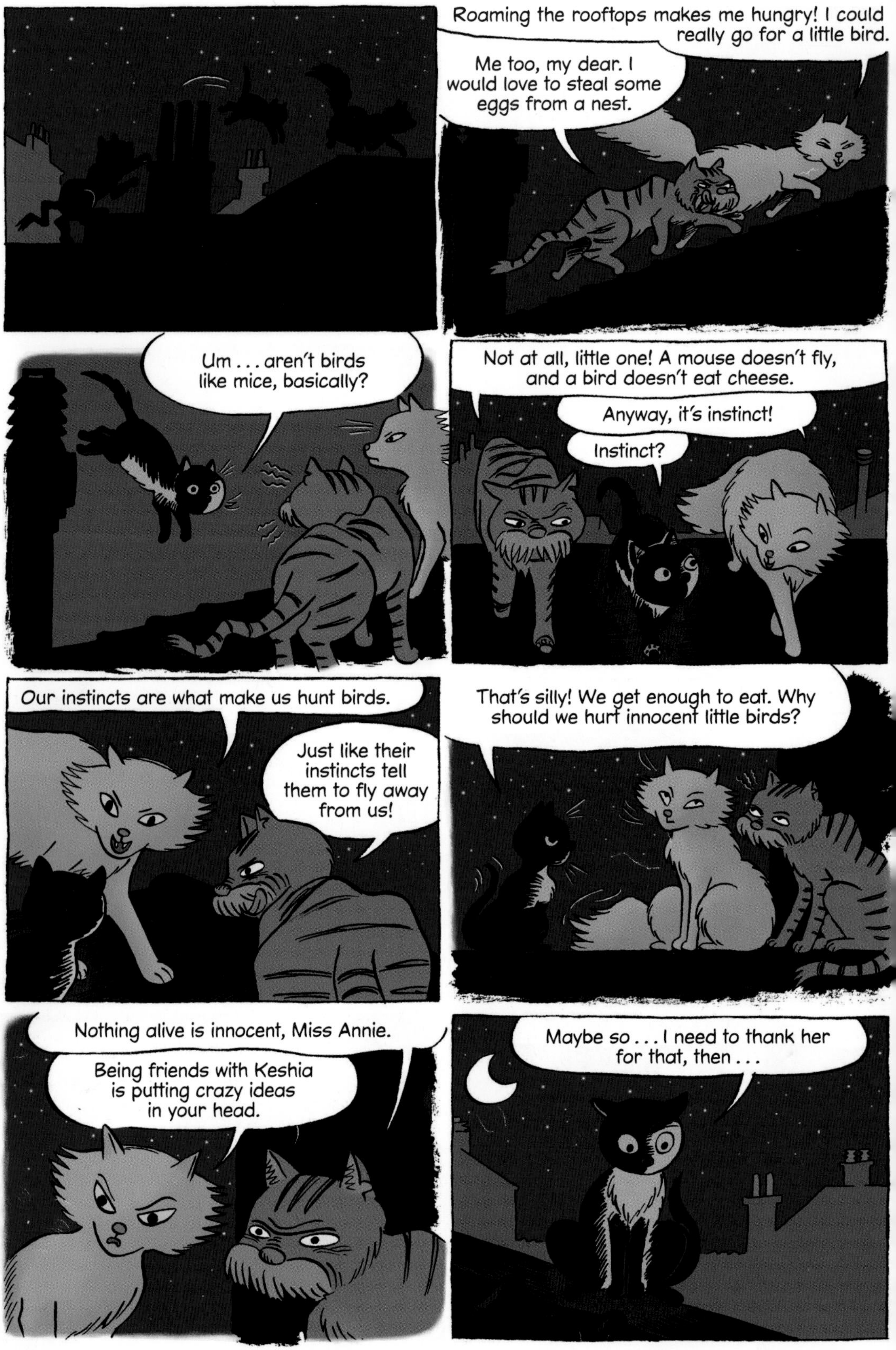
Roaming the rooftops makes me hungry! I could really go for a little bird.
Me too, my dear. I would love to steal some eggs from a nest.
Um . . . aren't birds like mice, basically?
Not at all, little one! A mouse doesn't fly, and a bird doesn't eat cheese.
Anyway, it's instinct!
Instinct?
Our instincts are what make us hunt birds.
Just like their instincts tell them to fly away from us!
That's silly! We get enough to eat. Why should we hurt innocent little birds?
Nothing alive is innocent, Miss Annie.
Being friends with Keshia is putting crazy ideas in your head.
Maybe so . . . I need to thank her for that, then . . .

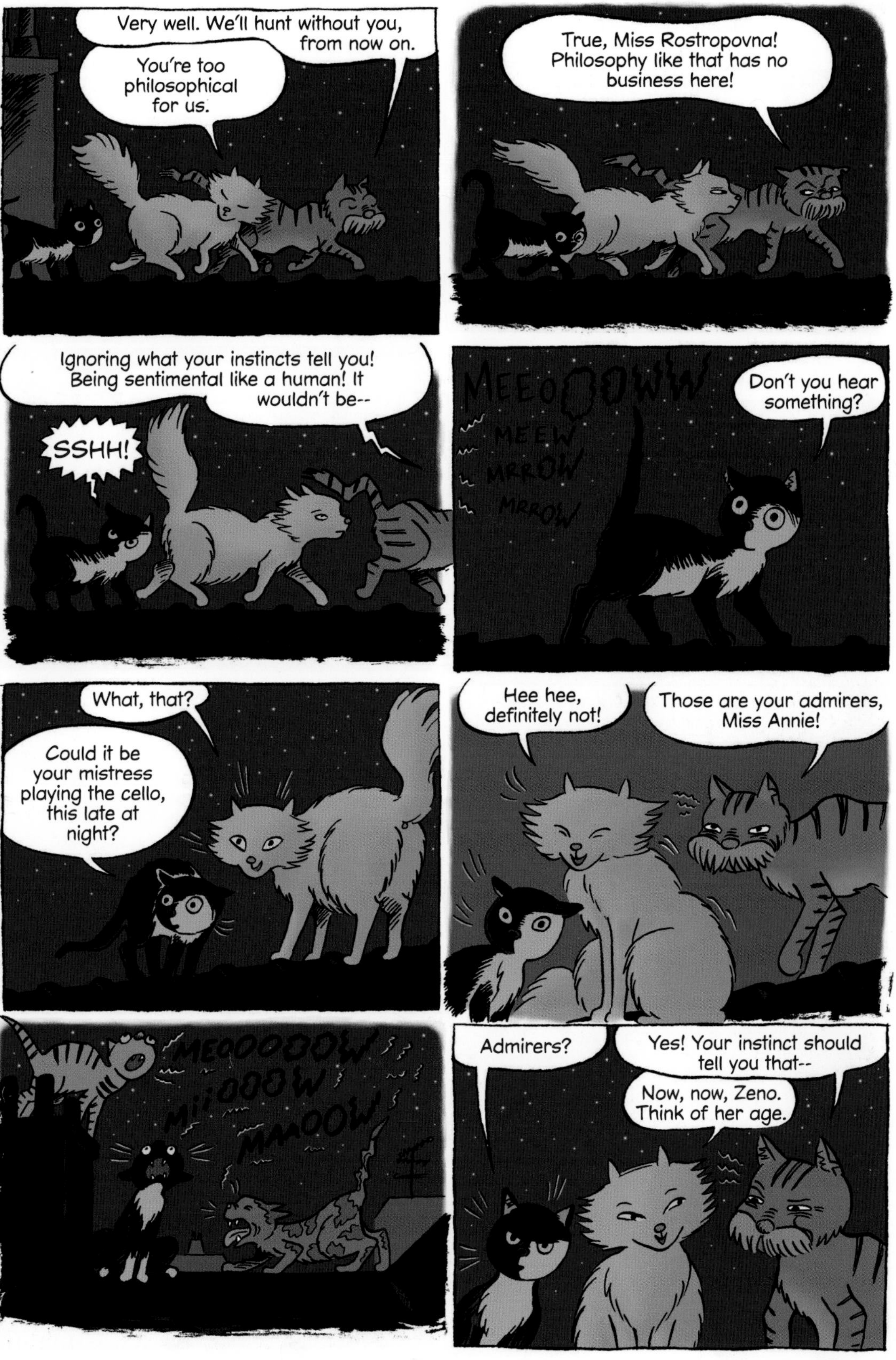

Very well. We'll hunt without you, from now on.
You're too philosophical for us.
True, Miss Rostropovna! Philosophy like that has no business here!
Ignoring what your instincts tell you! Being sentimental like a human! It wouldn't be--
SSHH!
MEEOOOWW
MEEW
MRROW
MRROW
Don't you hear something?
What, that?
Could it be your mistress playing the cello, this late at night?
Hee hee, definitely not!
Those are your admirers, Miss Annie!
MEOOOOOW
MIIOOOW
MAOOW
Admirers?
Yes! Your instinct should tell you that--
Now, now, Zeno. Think of her age.

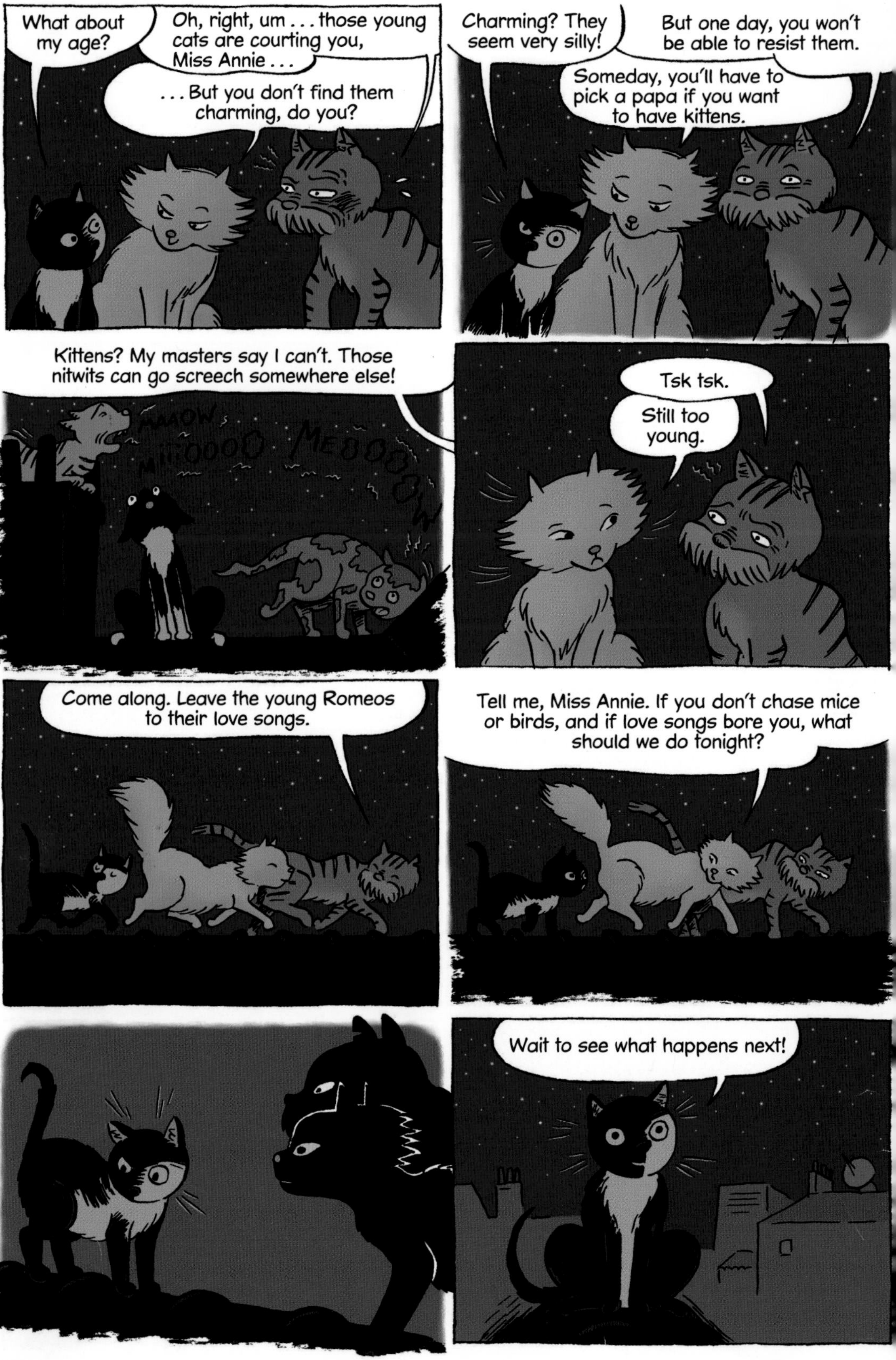
What about my age?
Oh, right, um . . . those young cats are courting you, Miss Annie . . .
. . . But you don't find them charming, do you?
Charming? They seem very silly!
But one day, you won't be able to resist them.
Someday, you'll have to pick a papa if you want to have kittens.
Kittens? My masters say I can't. Those nitwits can go screech somewhere else!
Tsk tsk.
Still too young.
Come along. Leave the young Romeos to their love songs.
Tell me, Miss Annie. If you don't chase mice or birds, and if love songs bore you, what should we do tonight?
Wait to see what happens next!

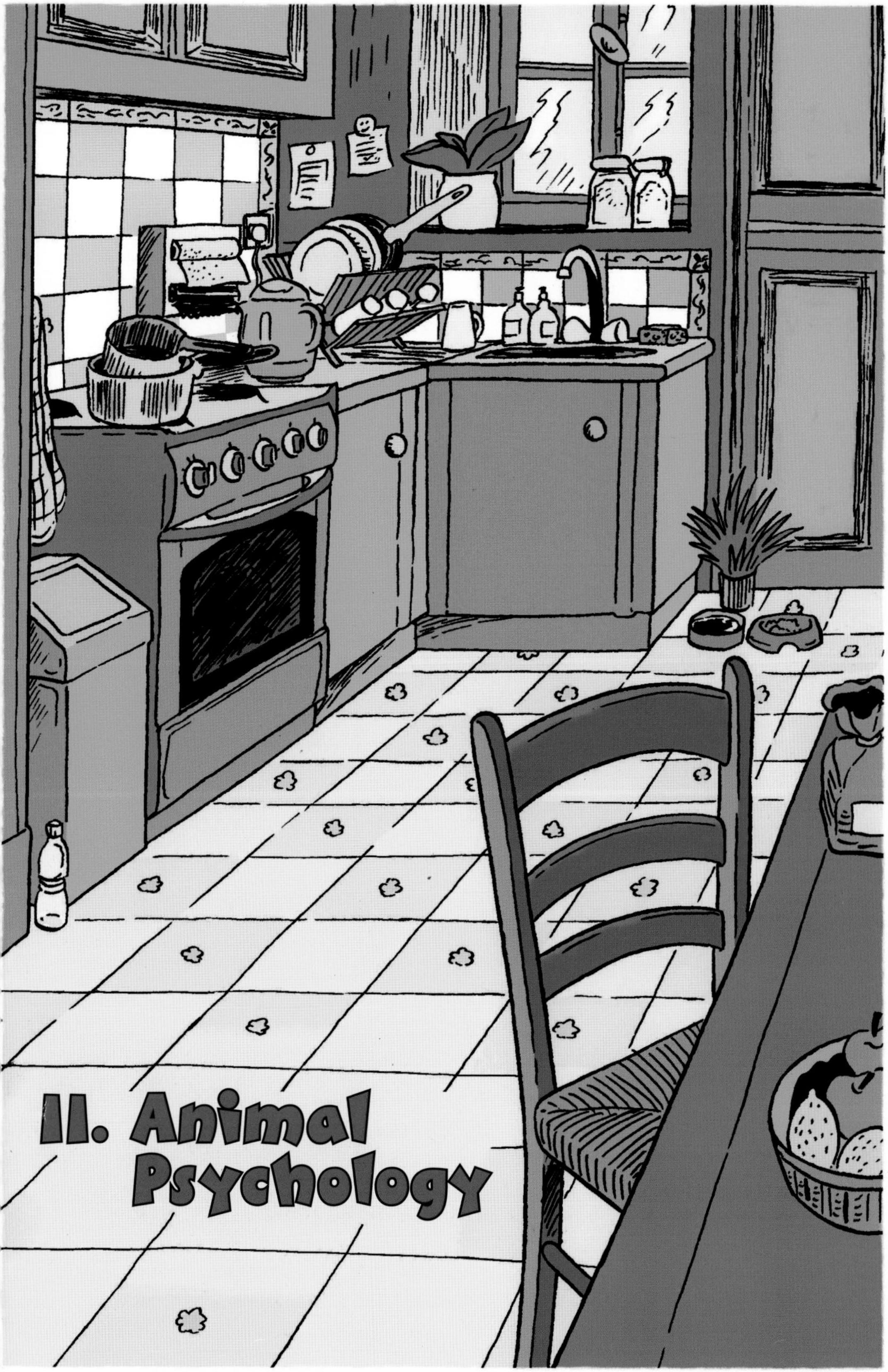
II. Animal Psychology

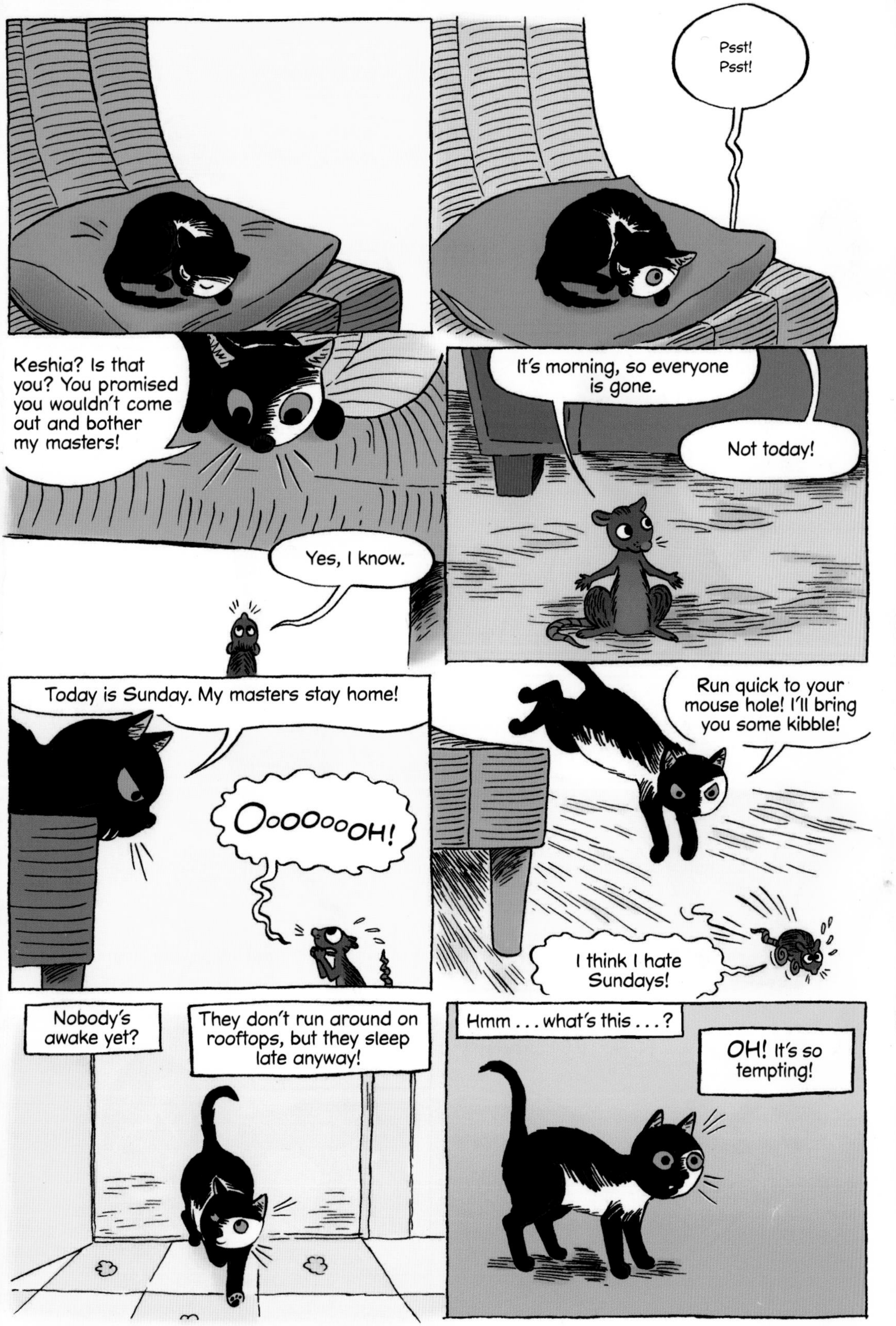

Psst!
Psst!
Keshia? Is that you? You promised you wouldn't come out and bother my masters!
It's morning, so everyone is gone.
Not today!
Yes, I know.
Today is Sunday. My masters stay home!
OoooooOH!
Run quick to your mouse hole! I'll bring you some kibble!
I think I hate Sundays!
Nobody's awake yet?
They don't run around on rooftops, but they sleep late anyway!
Hmm . . . what's this . . . ?
OH! It's so tempting!

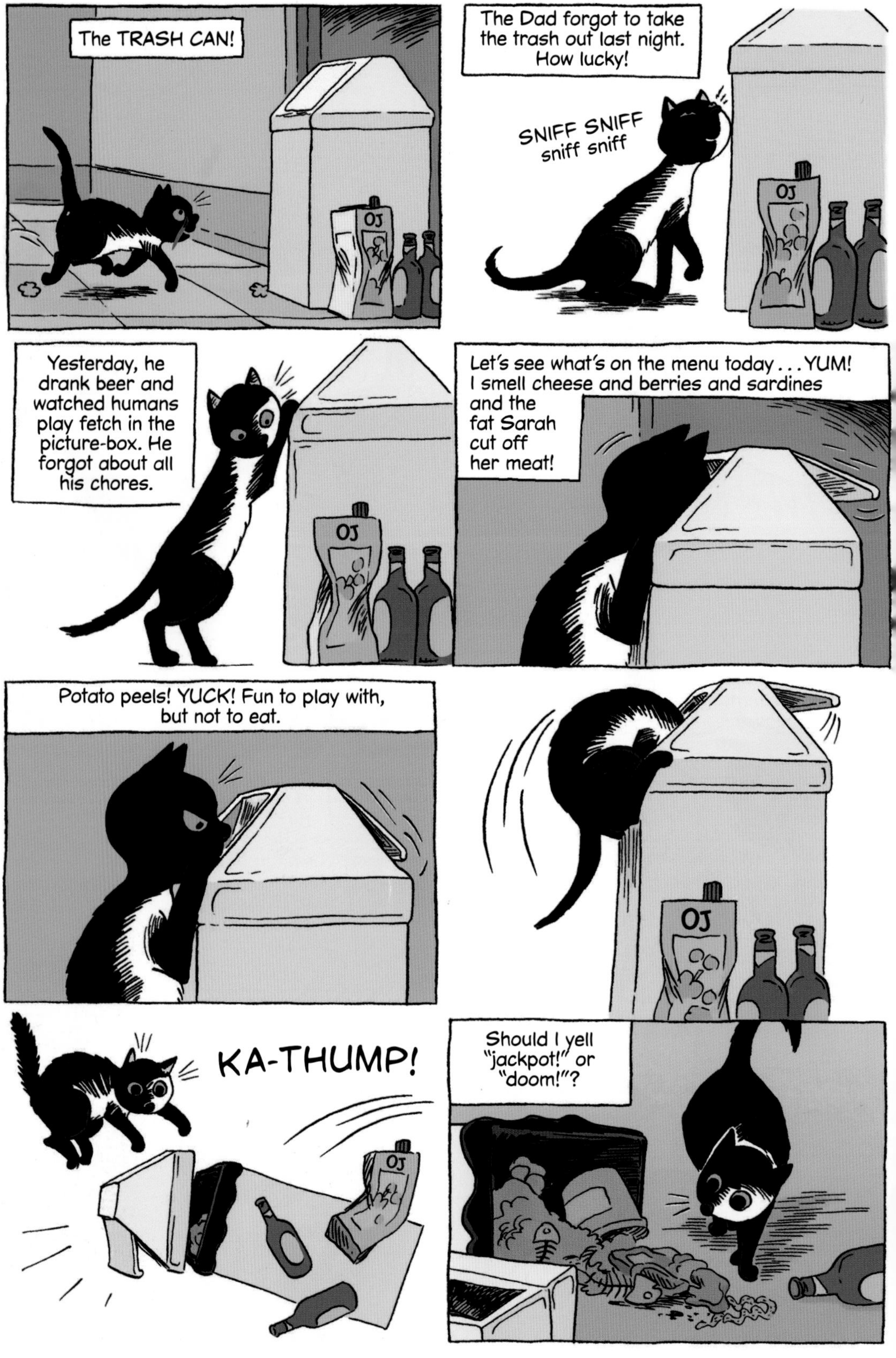

The TRASH CAN!
OJ
The Dad forgot to take the trash out last night. How lucky!
SNIFF SNIFF
sniff sniff
OJ
Yesterday, he drank beer and watched humans play fetch in the picture-box. He forgot about all his chores.
OJ
Let's see what's on the menu today . . . YUM! I smell cheese and berries and sardines and the fat Sarah cut off her meat!
Potato peels! YUCK! Fun to play with, but not to eat.
OJ
KA-THUMP!
OJ
Should I yell "jackpot!" or "doom!"?

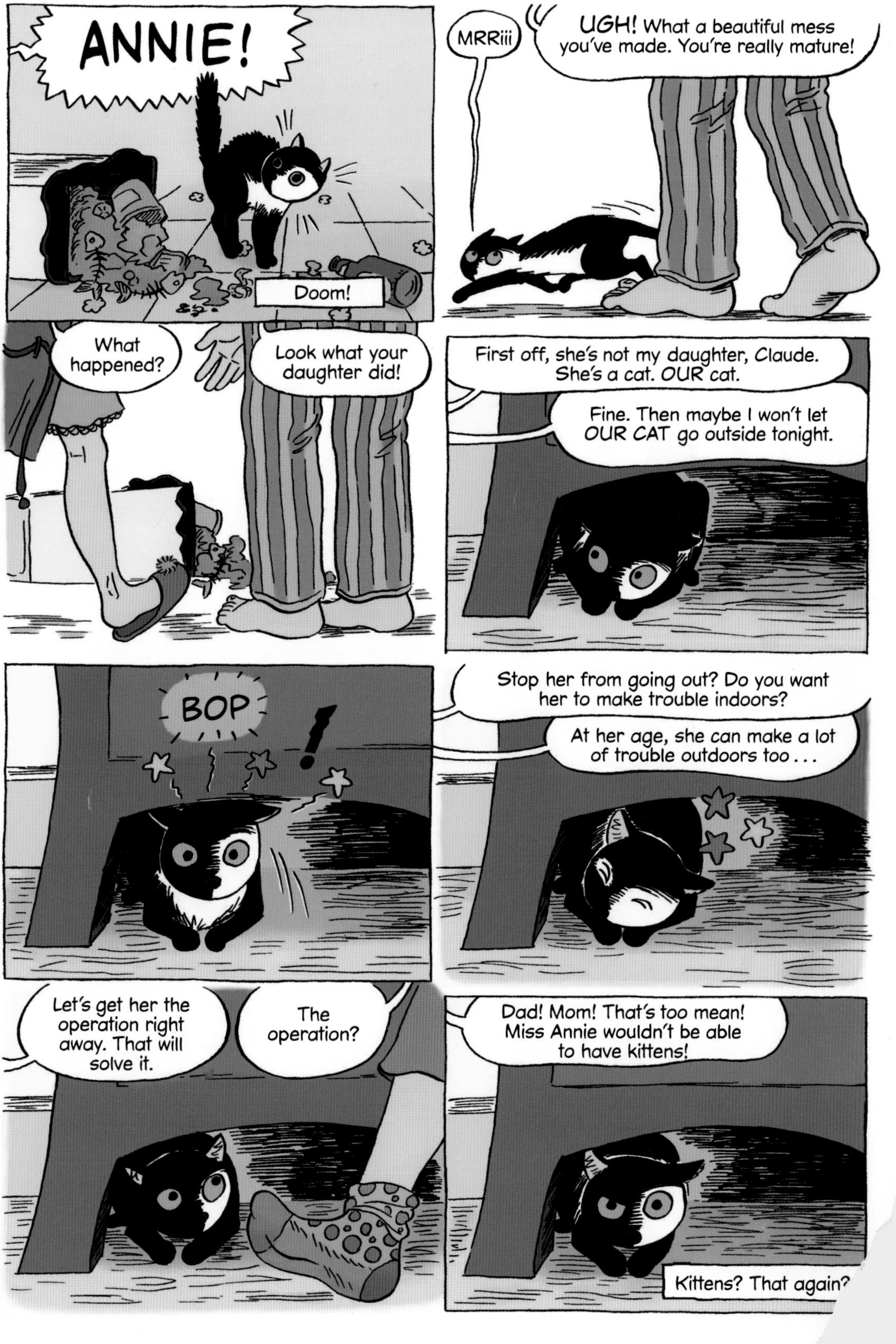
ANNIE!
Doom!
MRRiii
UGH! What a beautiful mess you've made. You're really mature!
What happened?
Look what your daughter did!
First off, she's not my daughter, Claude. She's a cat. OUR cat.
Fine. Then maybe I won't let OUR CAT go outside tonight.
BOP
Stop her from going out? Do you want her to make trouble indoors?
At her age, she can make a lot of trouble outdoors too . . .
Let's get her the operation right away. That will solve it.
The operation?
Dad! Mom! That's too mean! Miss Annie wouldn't be able to have kittens!
Kittens? That again?

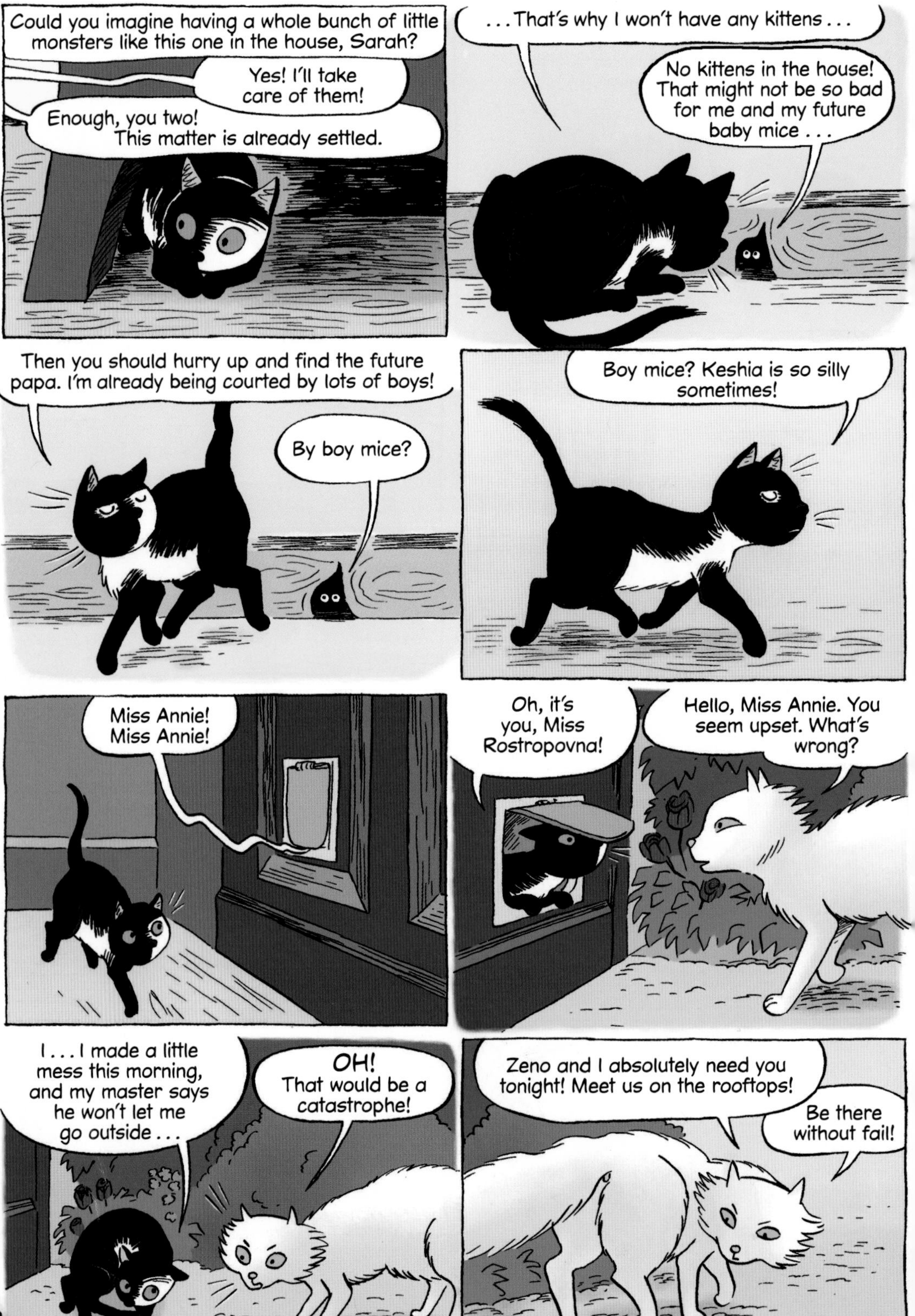
Could you imagine having a whole bunch of little monsters like this one in the house, Sarah?
Yes! I'll take care of them!
Enough, you two! This matter is already settled.
. . . That's why I won't have any kittens . . .
No kittens in the house! That might not be so bad for me and my future baby mice . . .
Then you should hurry up and find the future papa. I'm already being courted by lots of boys!
By boy mice?
Boy mice? Keshia is so silly sometimes!
Miss Annie! Miss Annie!
Oh, it's you, Miss Rostropovna!
Hello, Miss Annie. You seem upset. What's wrong?
I . . . I made a little mess this morning, and my master says he won't let me go outside . . .
OH! That would be a catastrophe!
Zeno and I absolutely need you tonight! Meet us on the rooftops!
Be there without fail!

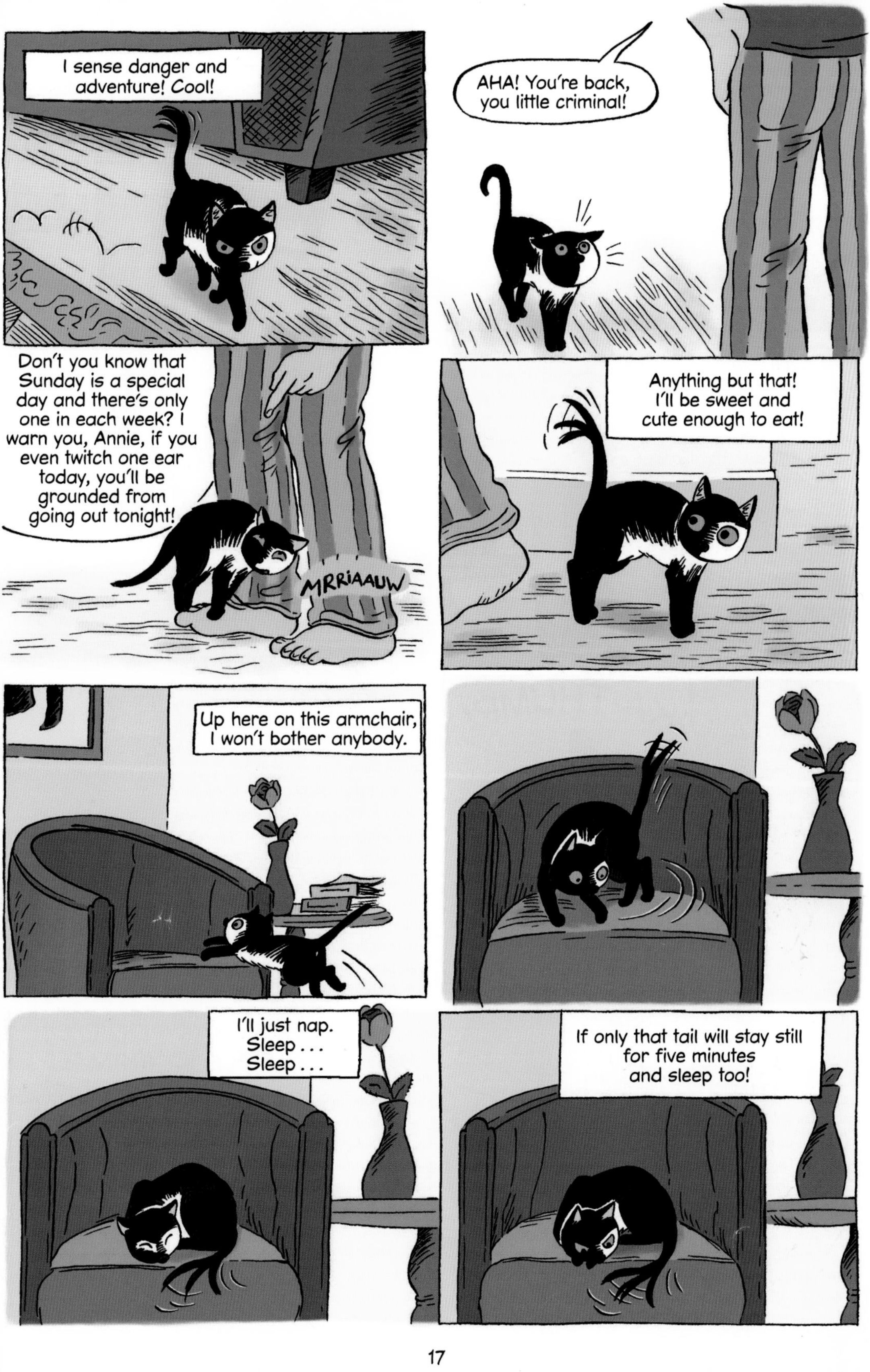
I sense danger and adventure! Cool!
AHA! You're back, you little criminal!
Don't you know that Sunday is a special day and there's only one in each week? I warn you, Annie, if you even twitch one ear today, you'll be grounded from going out tonight!
MRRIAAUW
Anything but that! I'll be sweet and cute enough to eat!
Up here on this armchair, I won't bother anybody.
I'll just nap. Sleep . . . Sleep . . .
If only that tail will stay still for five minutes and sleep too!

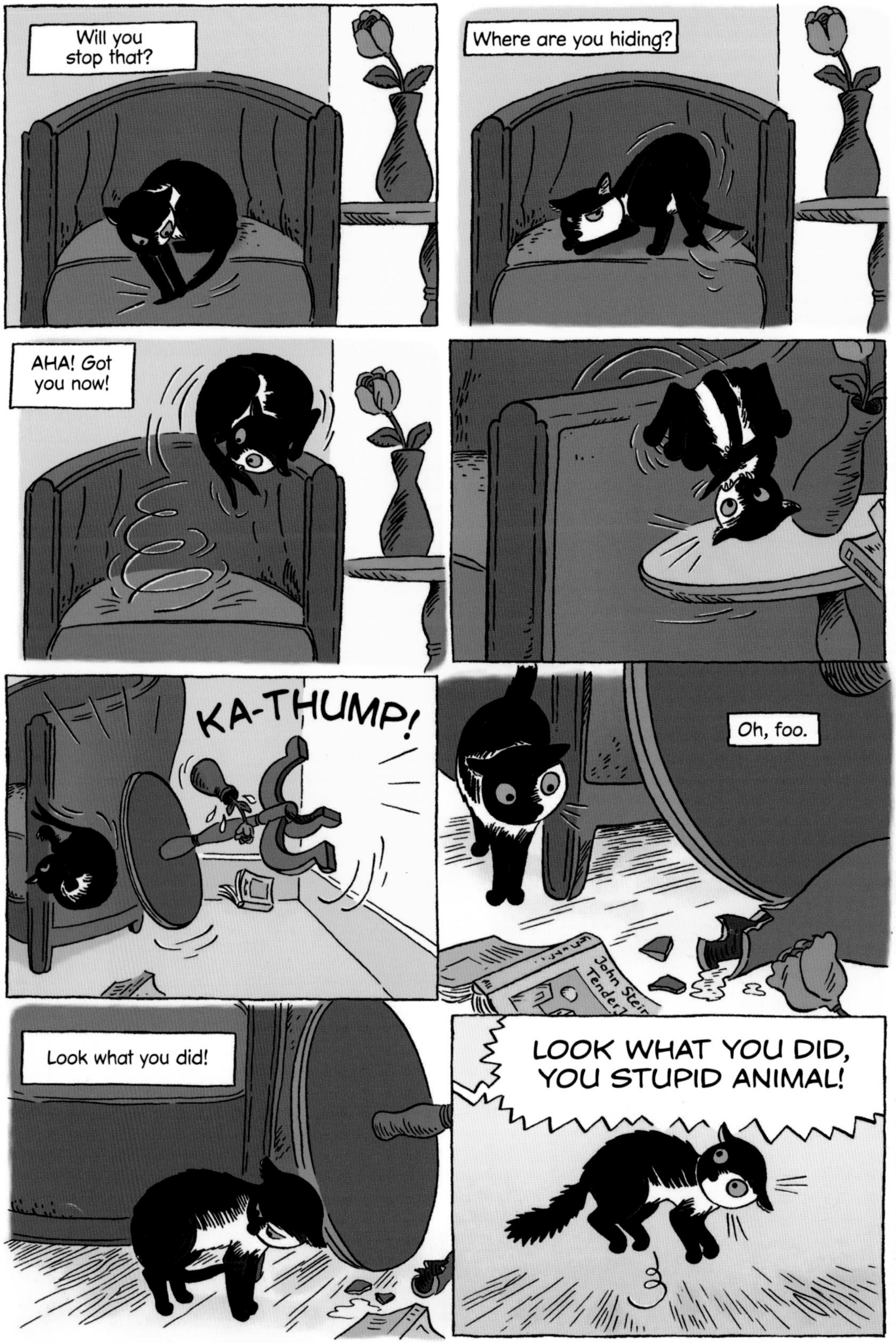

Will you stop that?
Where are you hiding?
AHA! Got you now!
KA-THUMP!
Oh, foo.
Look what you did!
LOOK WHAT YOU DID, YOU STUPID ANIMAL!

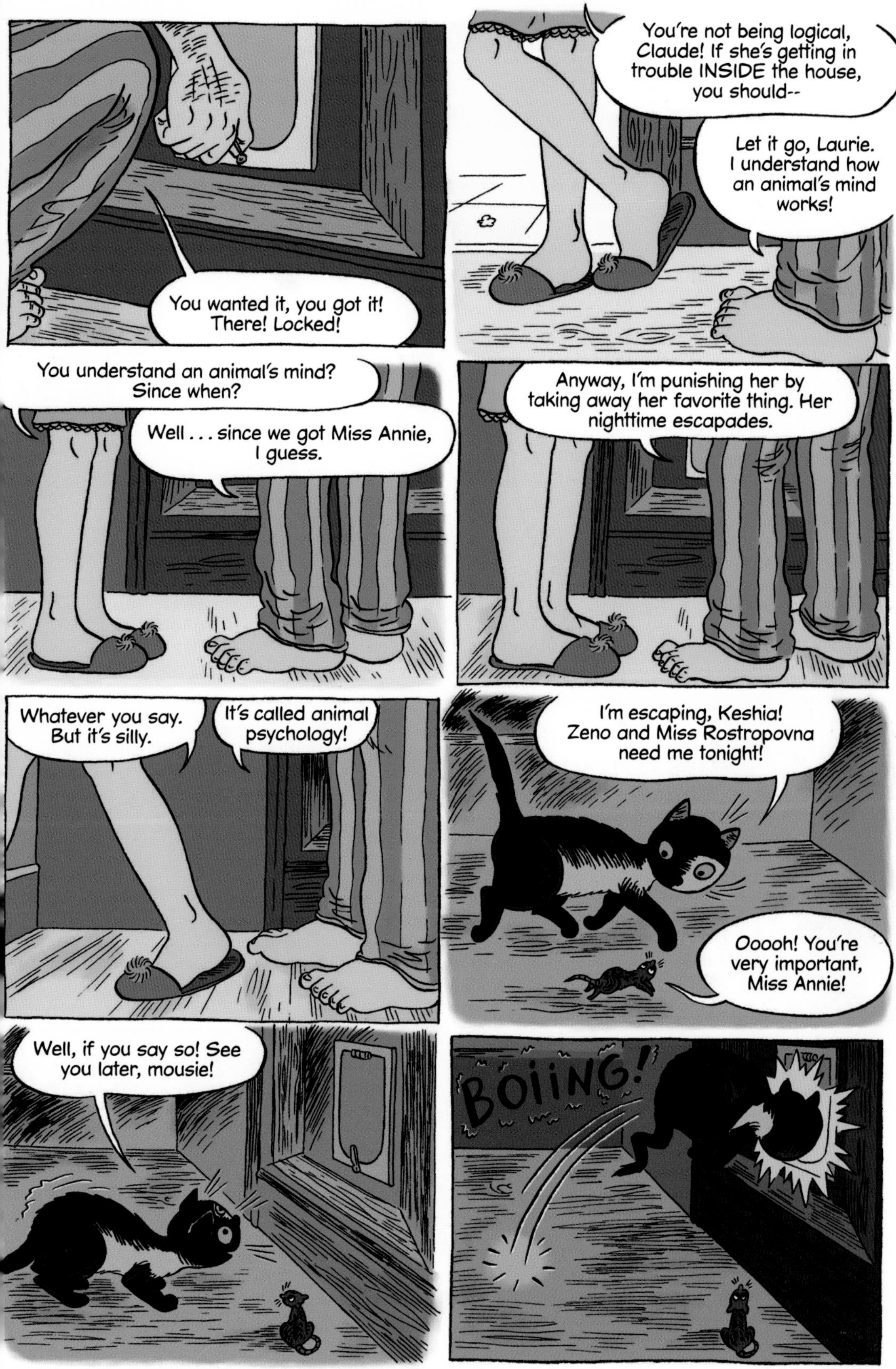
You wanted it, you got it! There! Locked!
You're not being logical, Claude! If she's getting in trouble INSIDE the house, you should--
Let it go, Laurie. I understand how an animal's mind works!
You understand an animal's mind? Since when?
Well . . . since we got Miss Annie, I guess.
Anyway, I'm punishing her by taking away her favorite thing. Her nighttime escapades.
Whatever you say. But it's silly.
It's called animal psychology!
I'm escaping, Keshia! Zeno and Miss Rostropovna need me tonight!
Ooooh! You're very important, Miss Annie!
Well, if you say so! See you later, mousie!
BOIING!

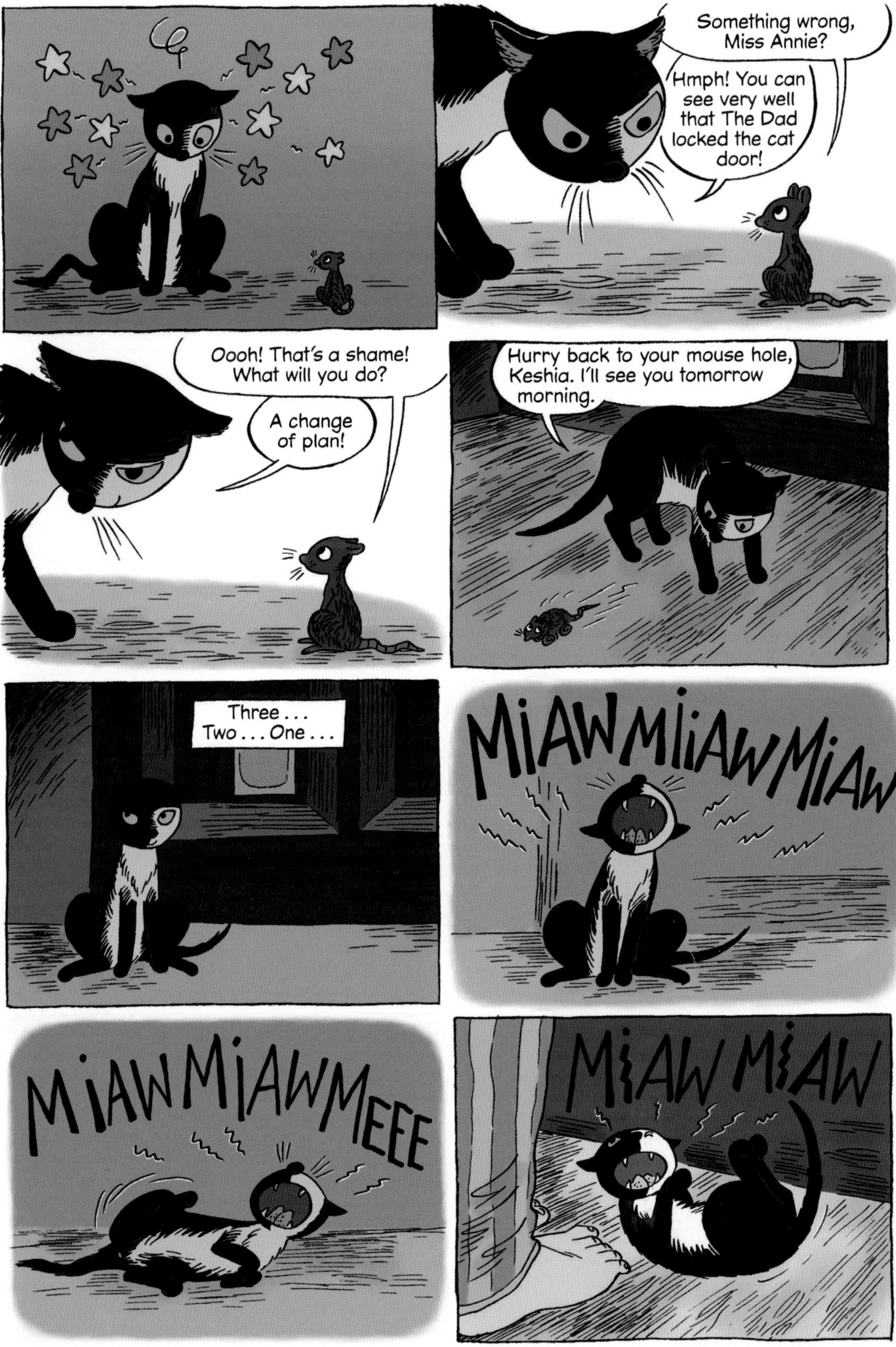
Something wrong, Miss Annie?
Hmph! You can see very well that The Dad locked the cat door!
Oooh! That's a shame! What will you do?
A change of plan!
Hurry back to your mouse hole, Keshia. I'll see you tomorrow morning.
Three . . . Two . . . One . . .
MIAW MIAW MIAW
MIAW MIAW MEEE
MIAW MIAW

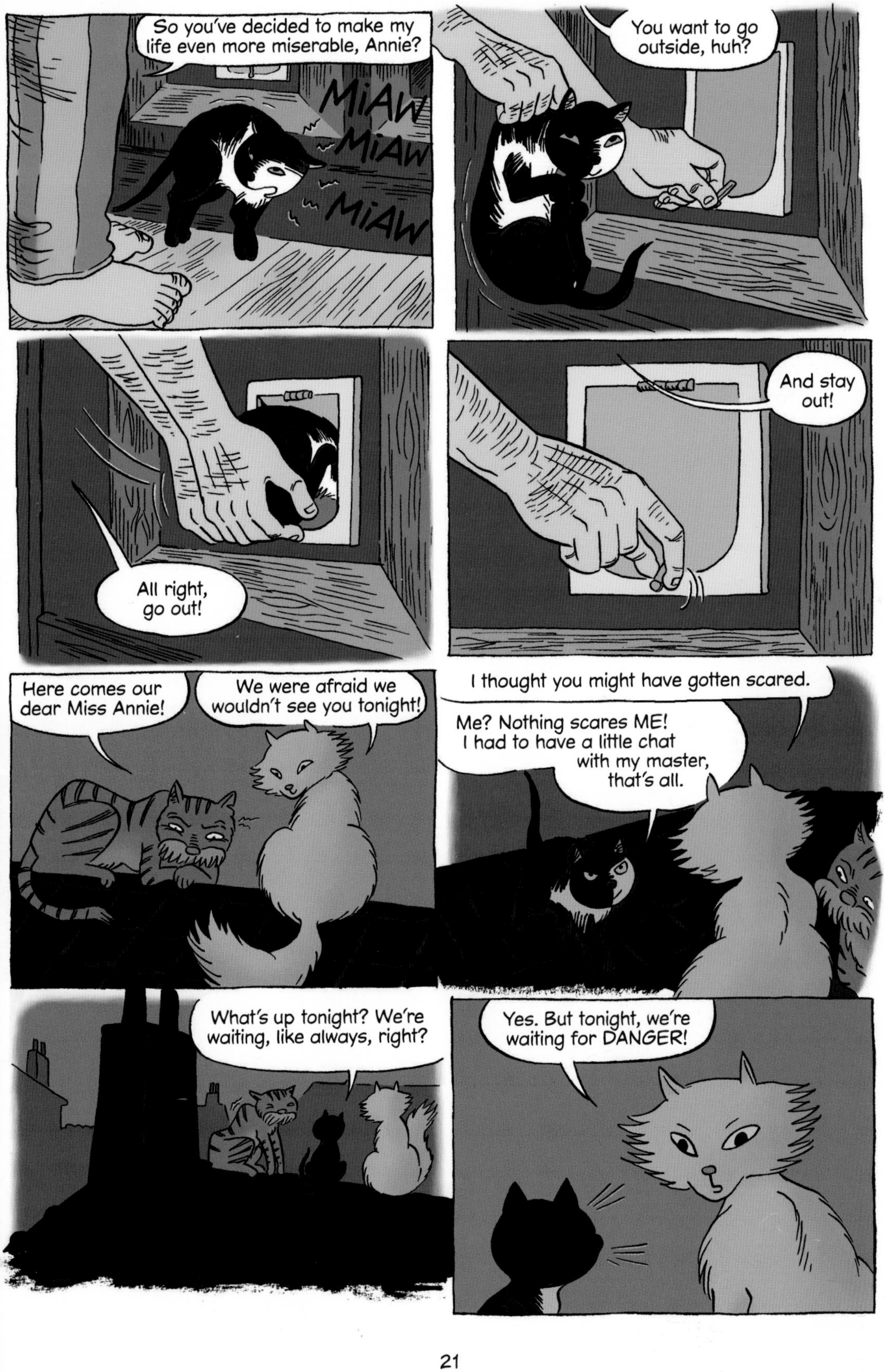

So you've decided to make my life even more miserable, Annie?
MiAW
MiAW
MiAW
You want to go outside, huh?
All right, go out!
And stay out!
Here comes our dear Miss Annie!
We were afraid we wouldn't see you tonight!
I thought you might have gotten scared.
Me? Nothing scares ME! I had to have a little chat with my master, that's all.
What's up tonight? We're waiting, like always, right?
Yes. But tonight, we're waiting for DANGER!

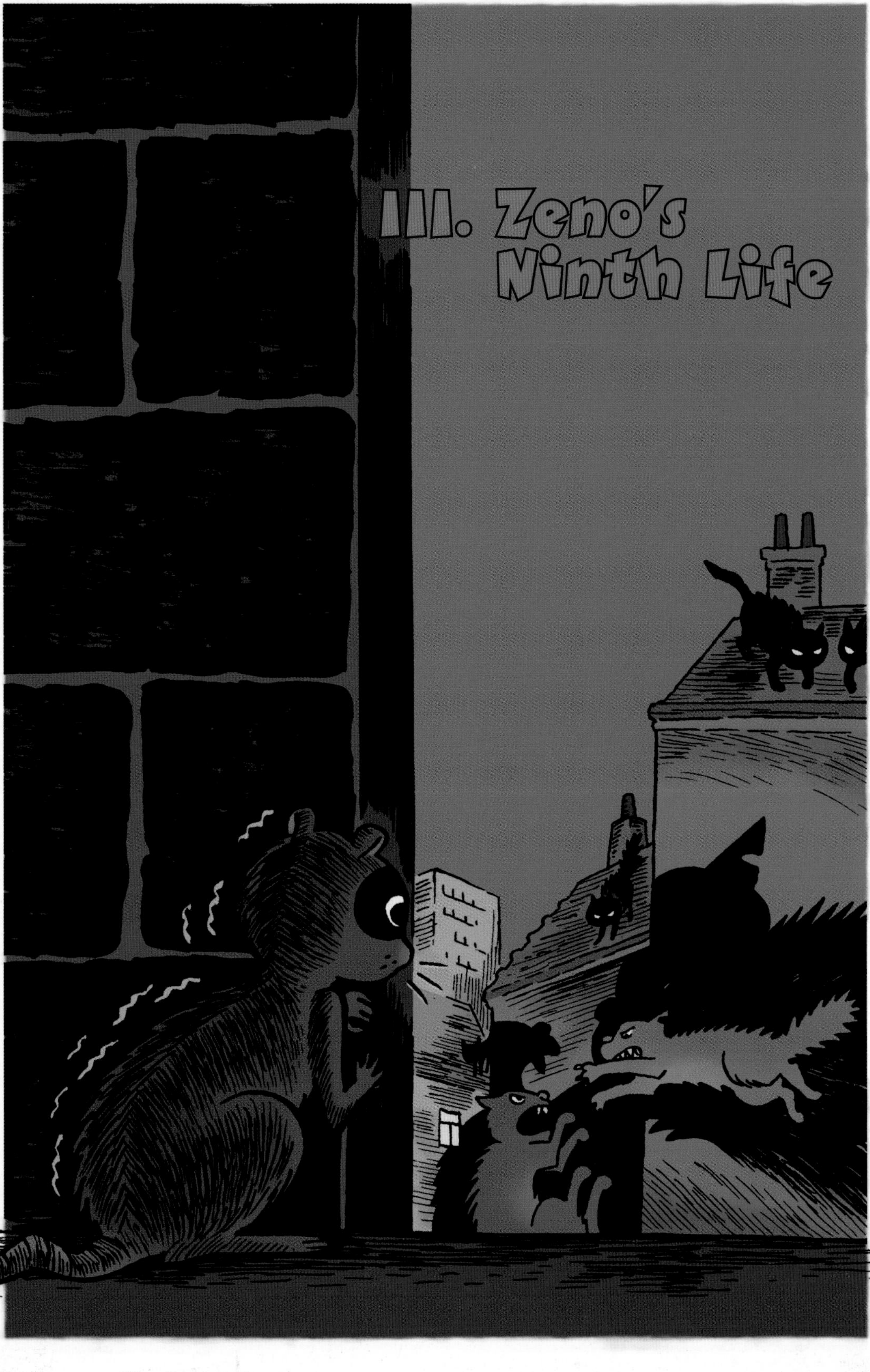
III. Zeno's
Ninth Life

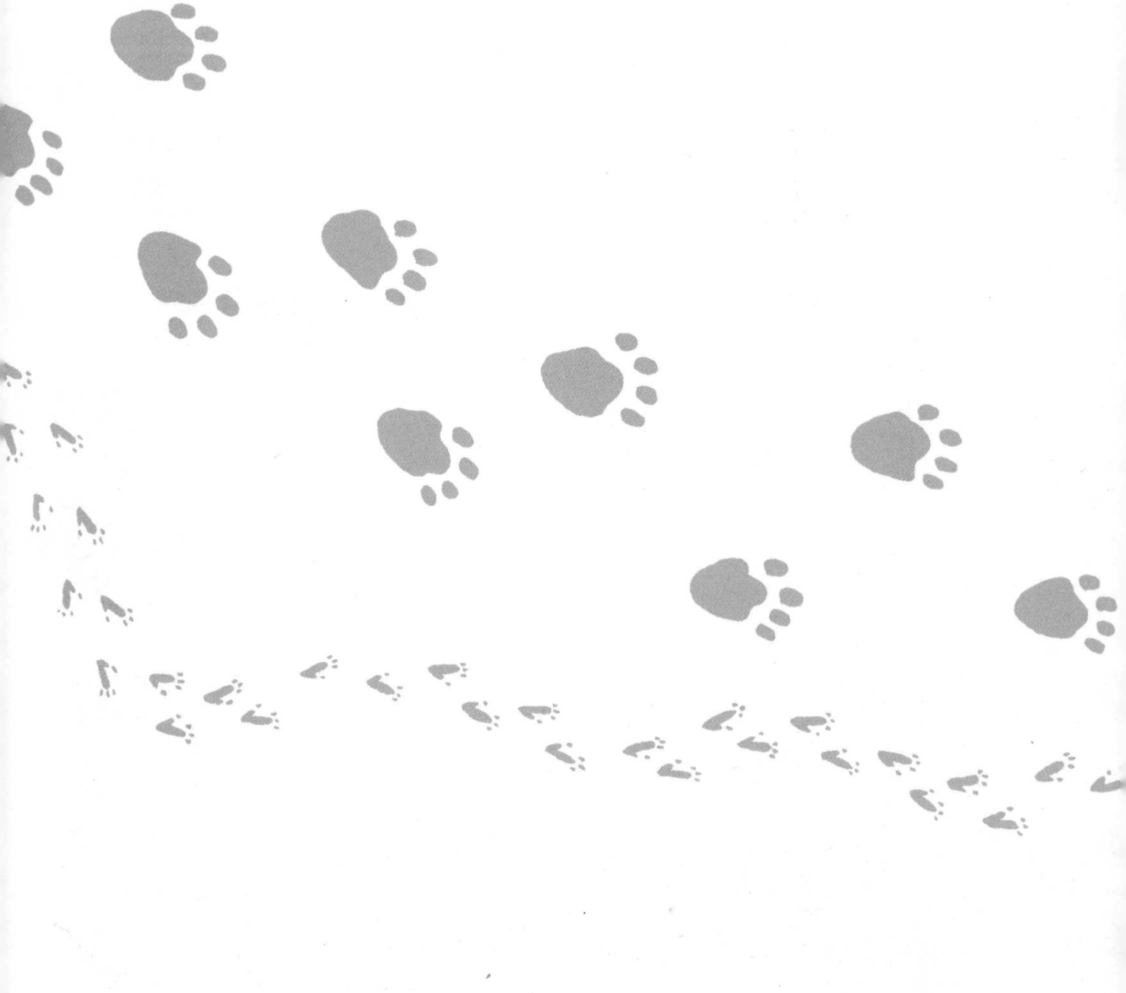

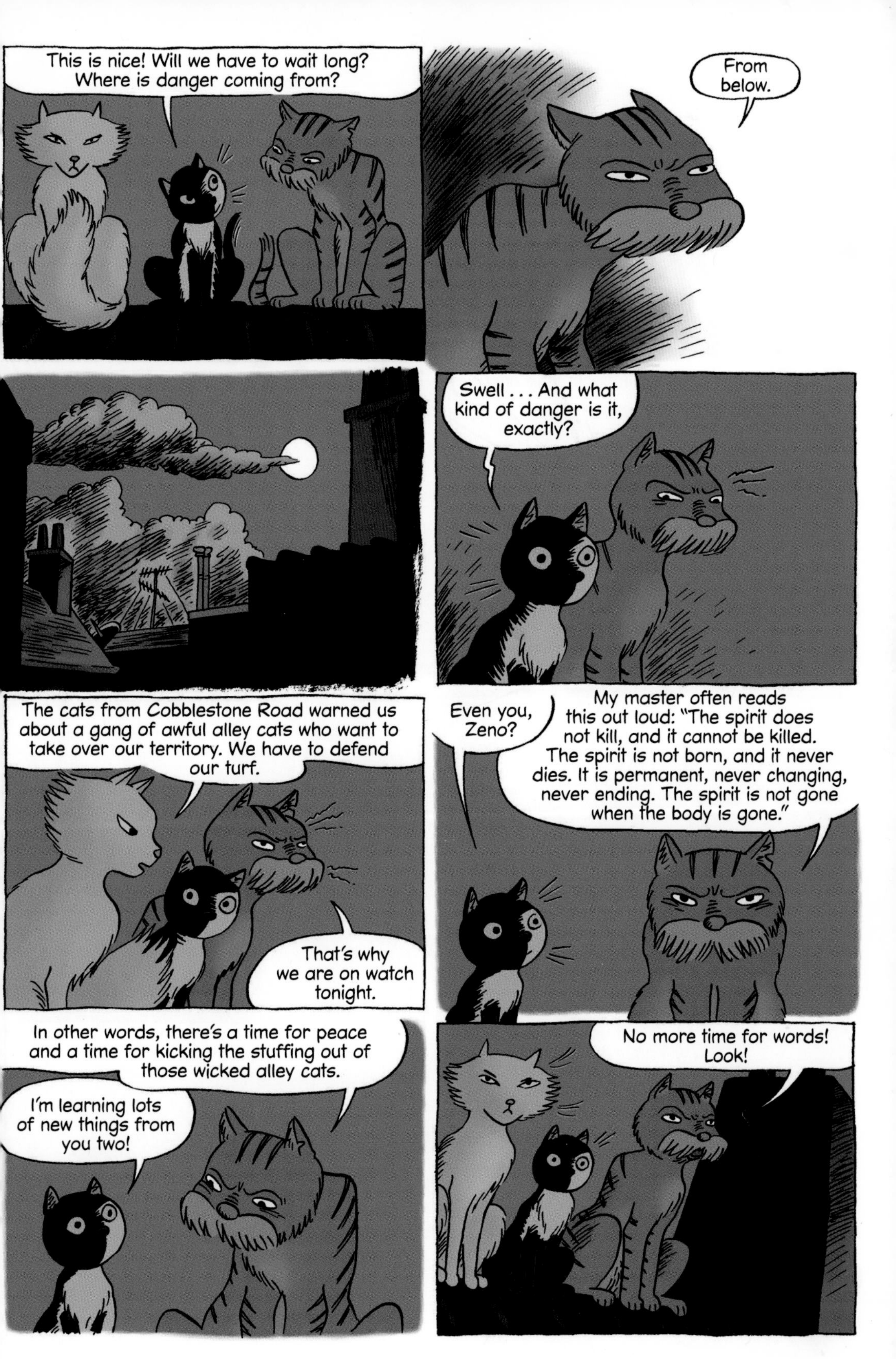
This is nice! Will we have to wait long? Where is danger coming from?
From below.
Swell . . . And what kind of danger is it, exactly?
The cats from Cobblestone Road warned us about a gang of awful alley cats who want to take over our territory. We have to defend our turf.
That's why we are on watch tonight.
Even you, Zeno?
My master often reads this out loud: "The spirit does not kill, and it cannot be killed. The spirit is not born, and it never dies. It is permanent, never changing, never ending. The spirit is not gone when the body is gone."
In other words, there's a time for peace and a time for kicking the stuffing out of those wicked alley cats.
I'm learning lots of new things from you two!
No more time for words! Look!

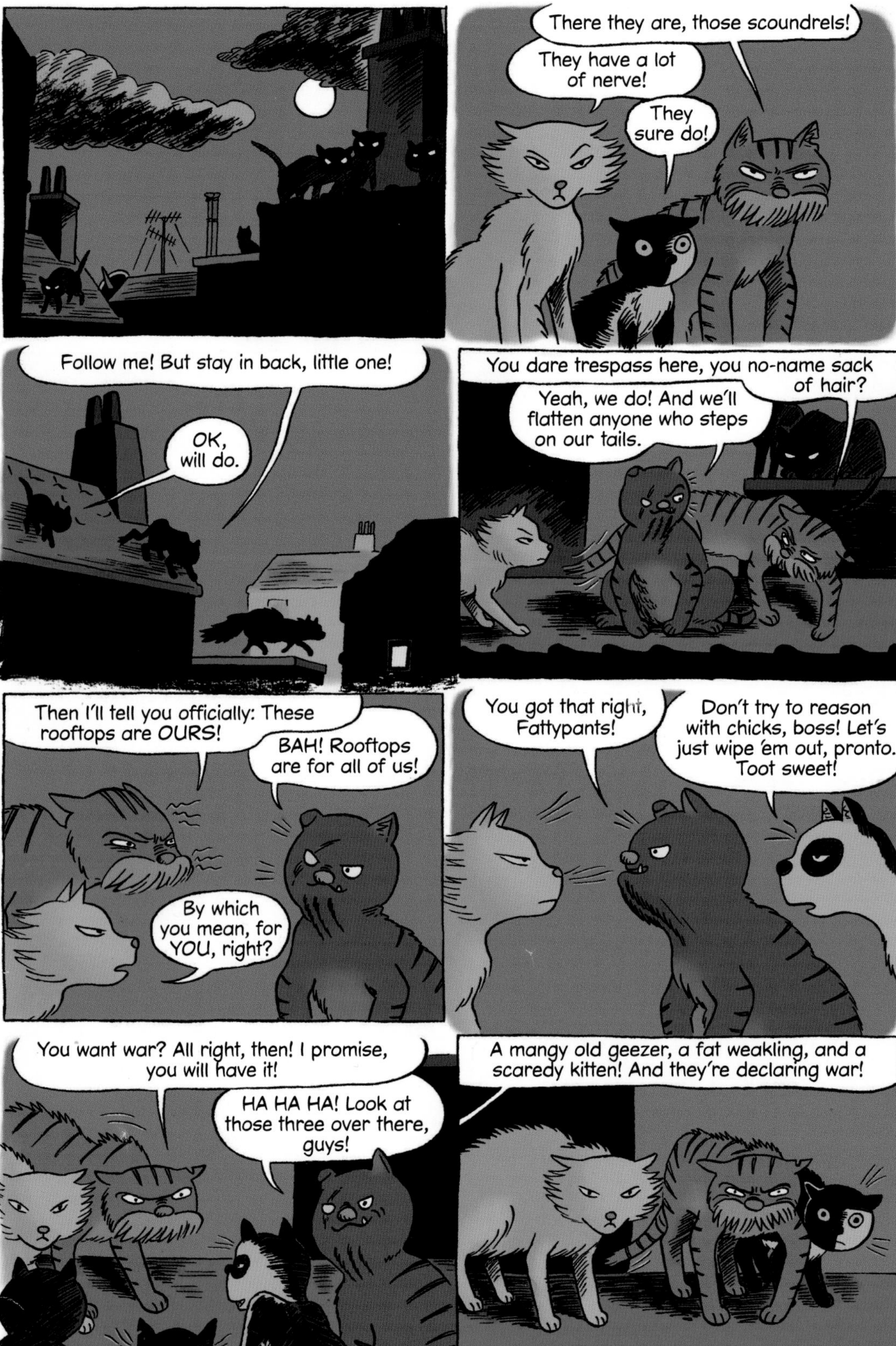
There they are, those scoundrels!
They have a lot of nerve!
They sure do!
Follow me! But stay in back, little one!
OK, will do.
You dare trespass here, you no-name sack of hair?
Yeah, we do! And we'll flatten anyone who steps on our tails.
Then I'll tell you officially: These rooftops are OURS!
BAH! Rooftops are for all of us!
By which you mean, for YOU, right?
You got that right, Fattypants!
Don't try to reason with chicks, boss! Let's just wipe 'em out, pronto. Toot sweet!
You want war? All right, then! I promise, you will have it!
HA HA HA! Look at those three over there, guys!
A mangy old geezer, a fat weakling, and a scaredy kitten! And they're declaring war!

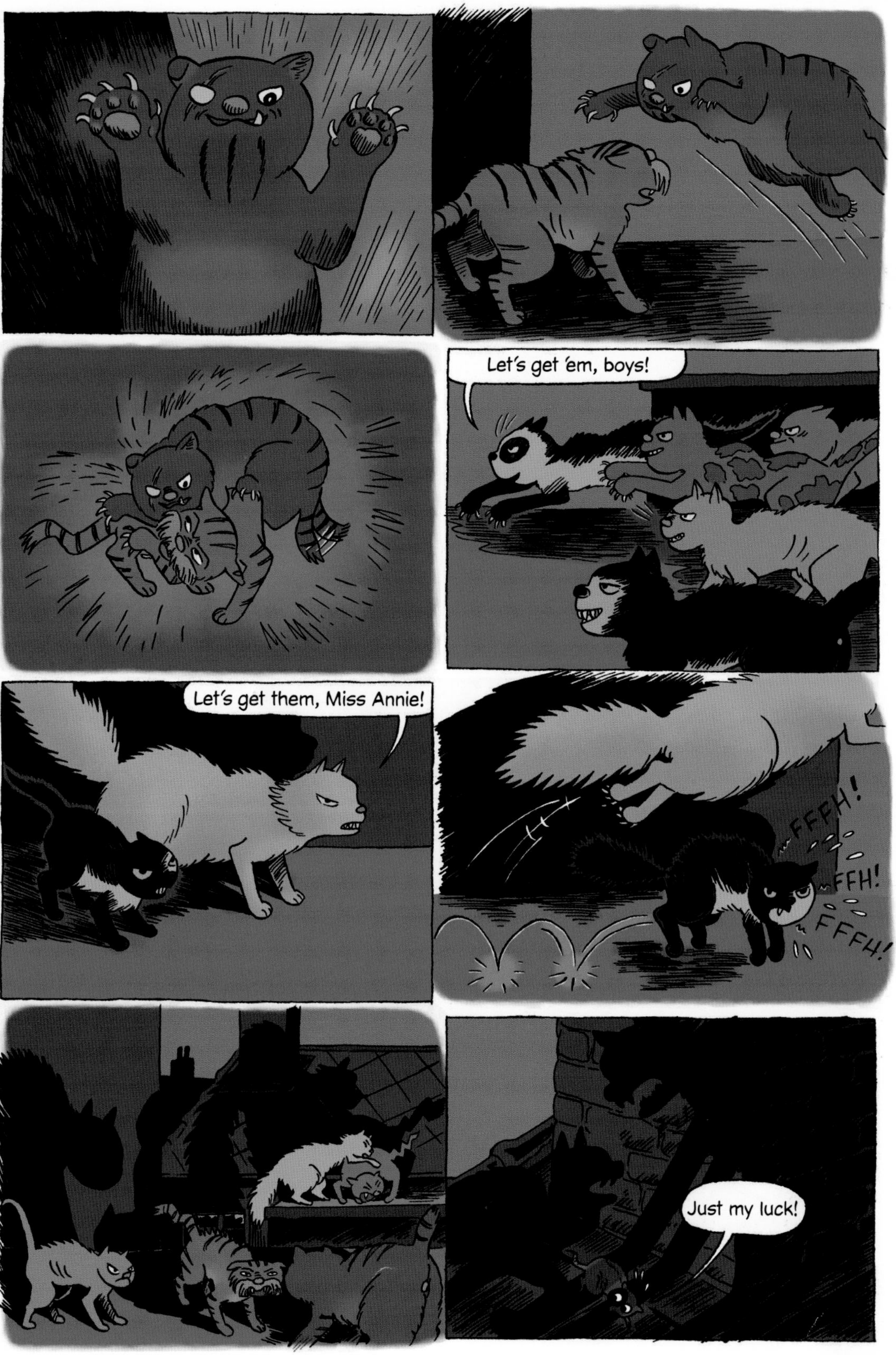
Let's get 'em, boys!
Let's get them, Miss Annie!
FFFH!
FFH!
FFFH!
Just my luck!

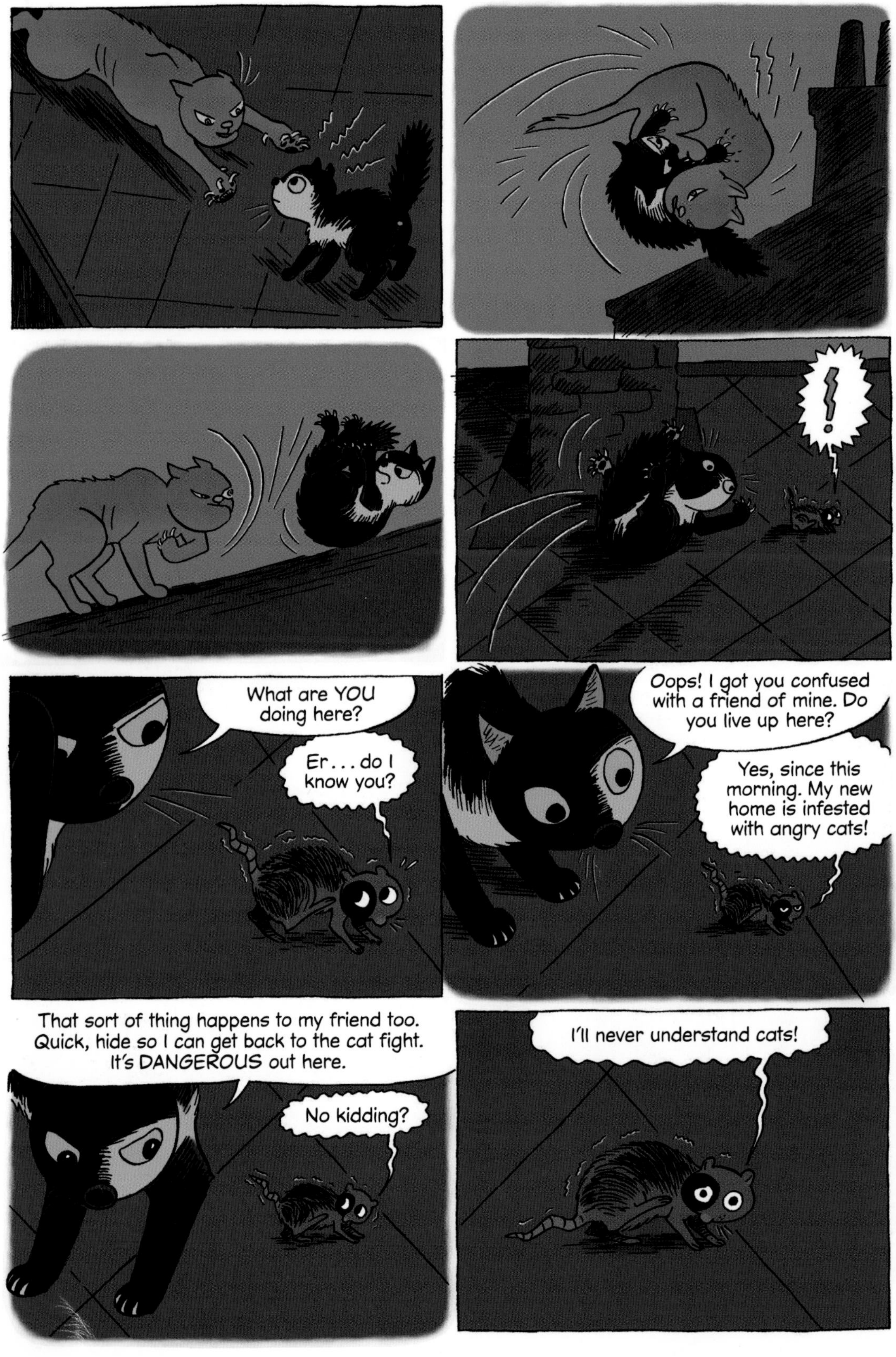

!
What are YOU doing here?
Er . . . do I know you?
Oops! I got you confused with a friend of mine. Do you live up here?
Yes, since this morning. My new home is infested with angry cats!
That sort of thing happens to my friend too. Quick, hide so I can get back to the cat fight. It's DANGEROUS out here.
No kidding?
I'll never understand cats!

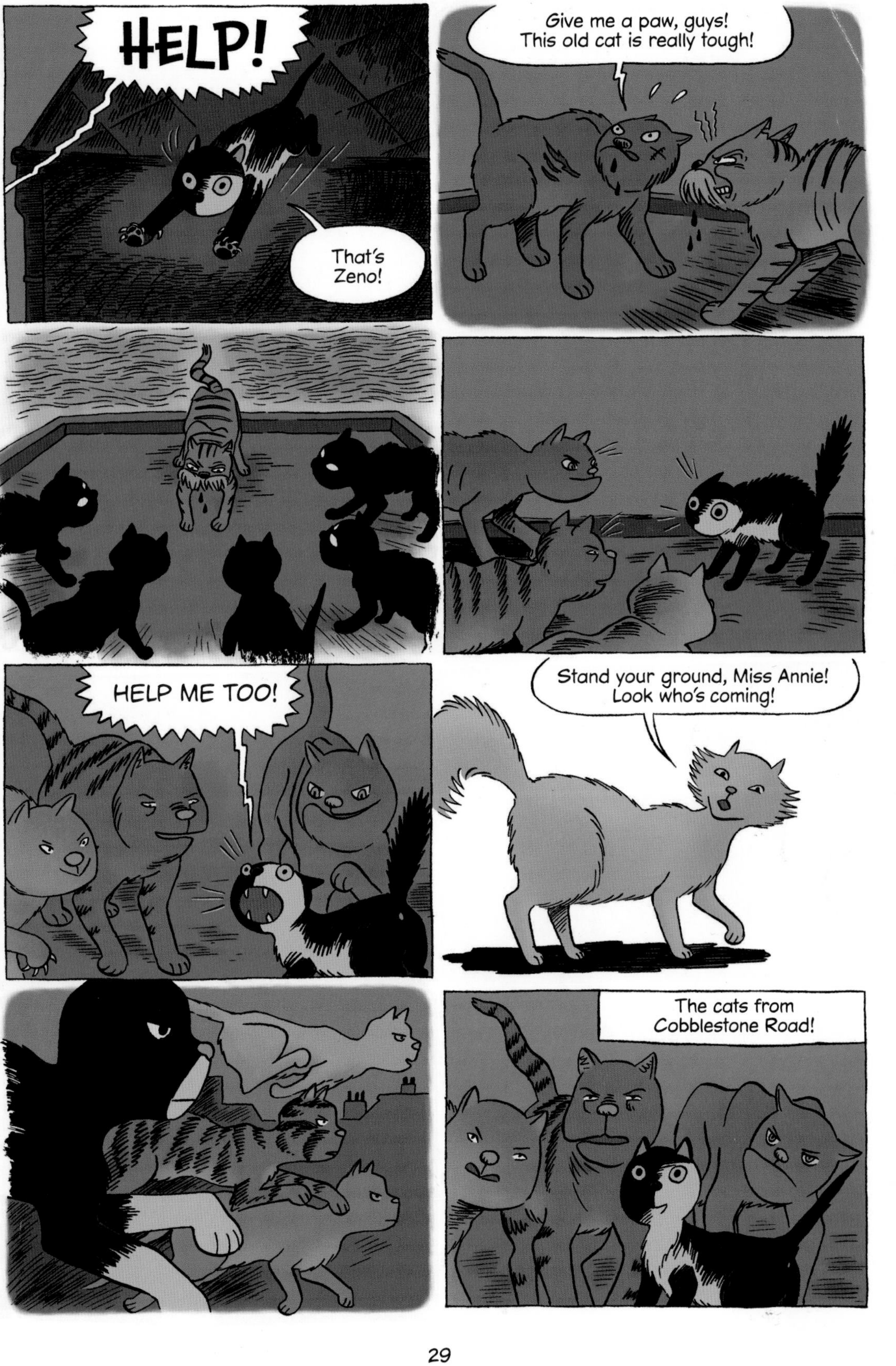
HELP!
That's Zeno!
Give me a paw, guys! This old cat is really tough!
HELP ME TOO!
Stand your ground, Miss Annie! Look who's coming!
The cats from Cobblestone Road!

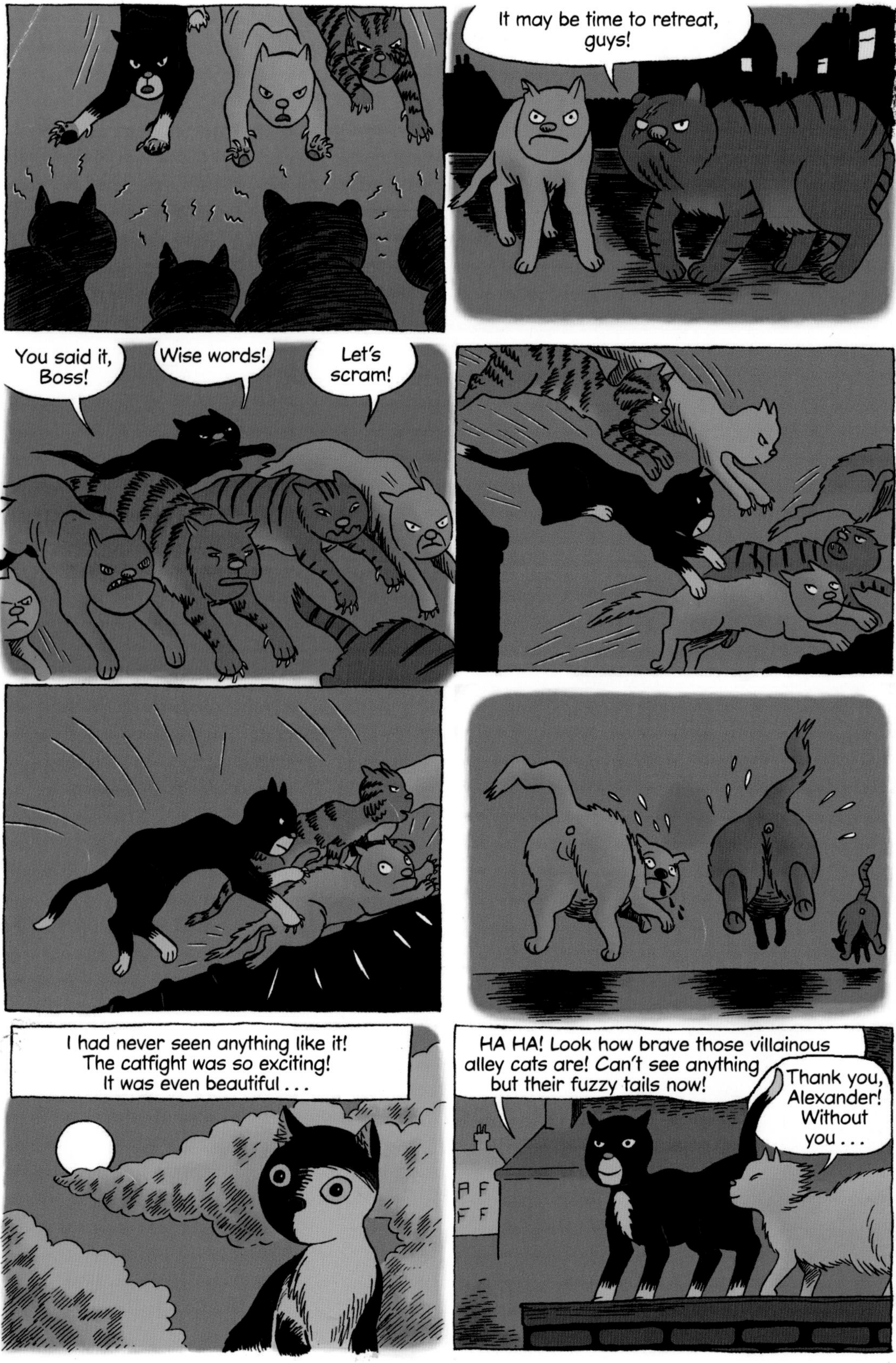
It may be time to retreat, guys!
You said it, Boss!
Wise words!
Let's scram!
I had never seen anything like it! The catfight was so exciting! It was even beautiful . . .
HA HA! Look how brave those villainous alley cats are! Can't see anything but their fuzzy tails now!
Thank you, Alexander! Without you . . .

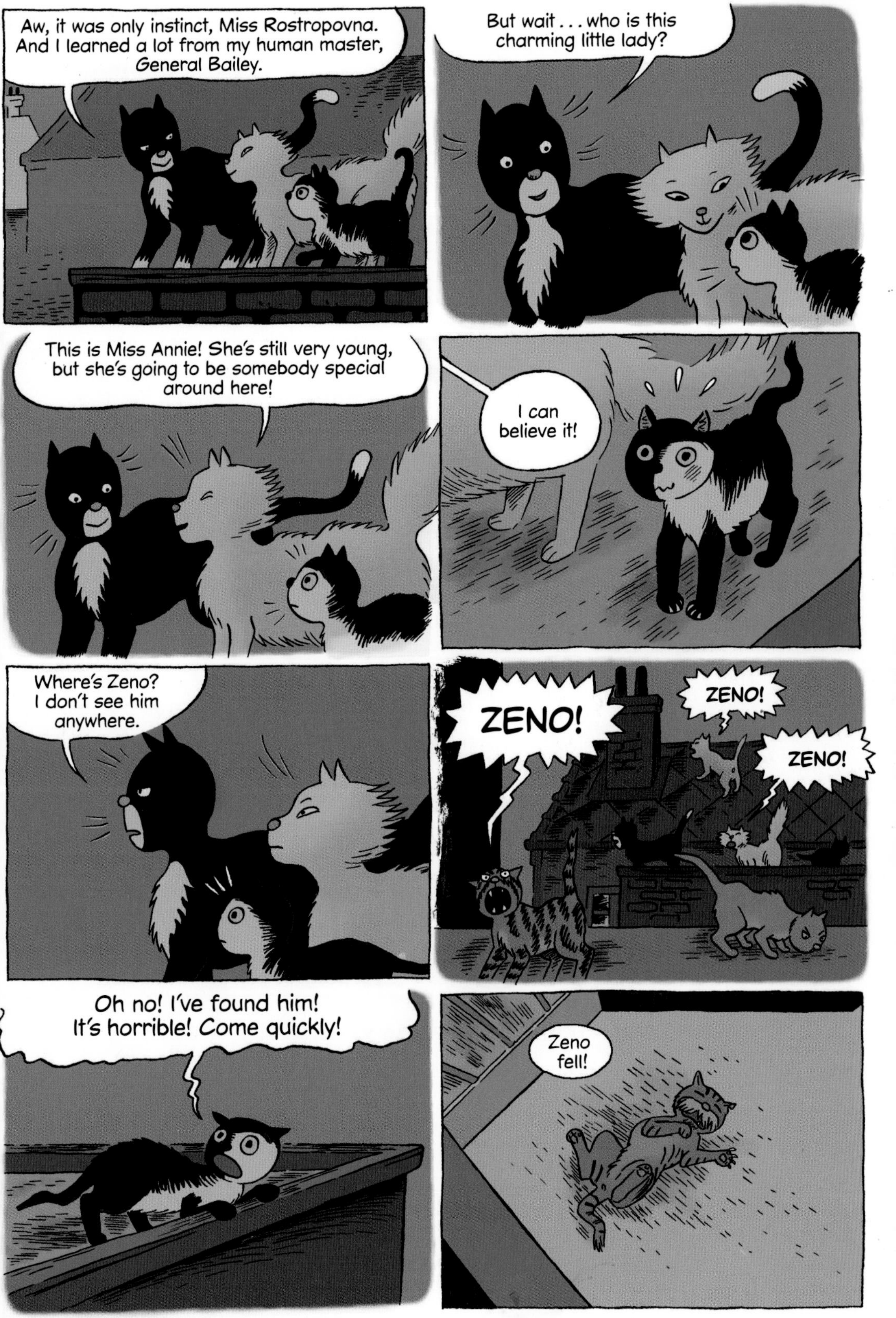
Aw, it was only instinct, Miss Rostropovna. And I learned a lot from my human master, General Bailey.
But wait . . . who is this charming little lady?
This is Miss Annie! She's still very young, but she's going to be somebody special around here!
I can believe it!
Where's Zeno? I don't see him anywhere.
ZENO!
ZENO!
ZENO!
Oh no! I've found him! It's horrible! Come quickly!
Zeno fell!

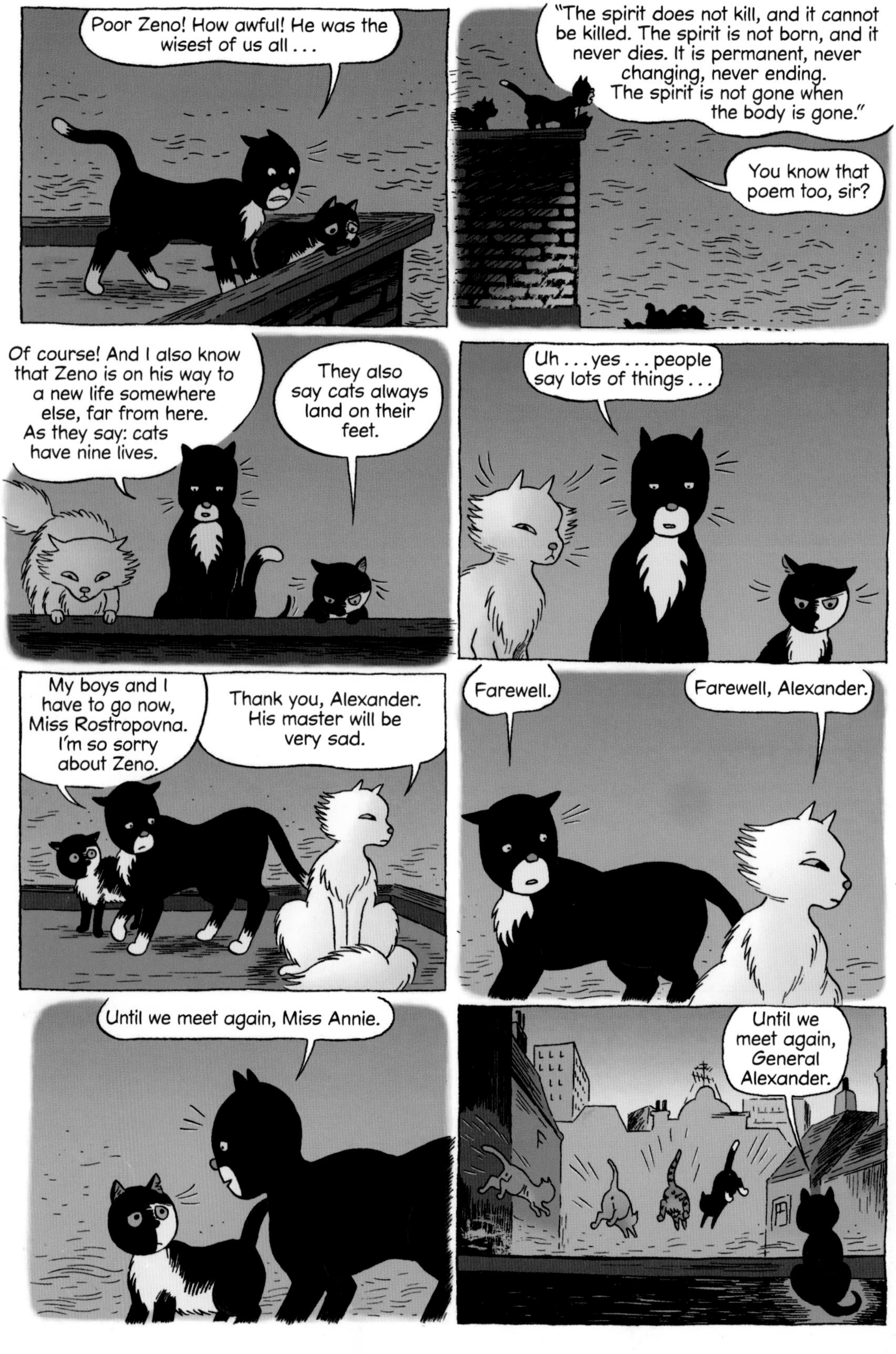

Poor Zeno! How awful! He was the wisest of us all . . .
"The spirit does not kill, and it cannot be killed. The spirit is not born, and it never dies. It is permanent, never changing, never ending. The spirit is not gone when the body is gone."
You know that poem too, sir?
Of course! And I also know that Zeno is on his way to a new life somewhere else, far from here. As they say: cats have nine lives.
They also say cats always land on their feet.
Uh . . . yes . . . people say lots of things . . .
My boys and I have to go now, Miss Rostropovna. I'm so sorry about Zeno.
Thank you, Alexander. His master will be very sad.
Farewell.
Farewell, Alexander.
Until we meet again, Miss Annie.
Until we meet again, General Alexander.

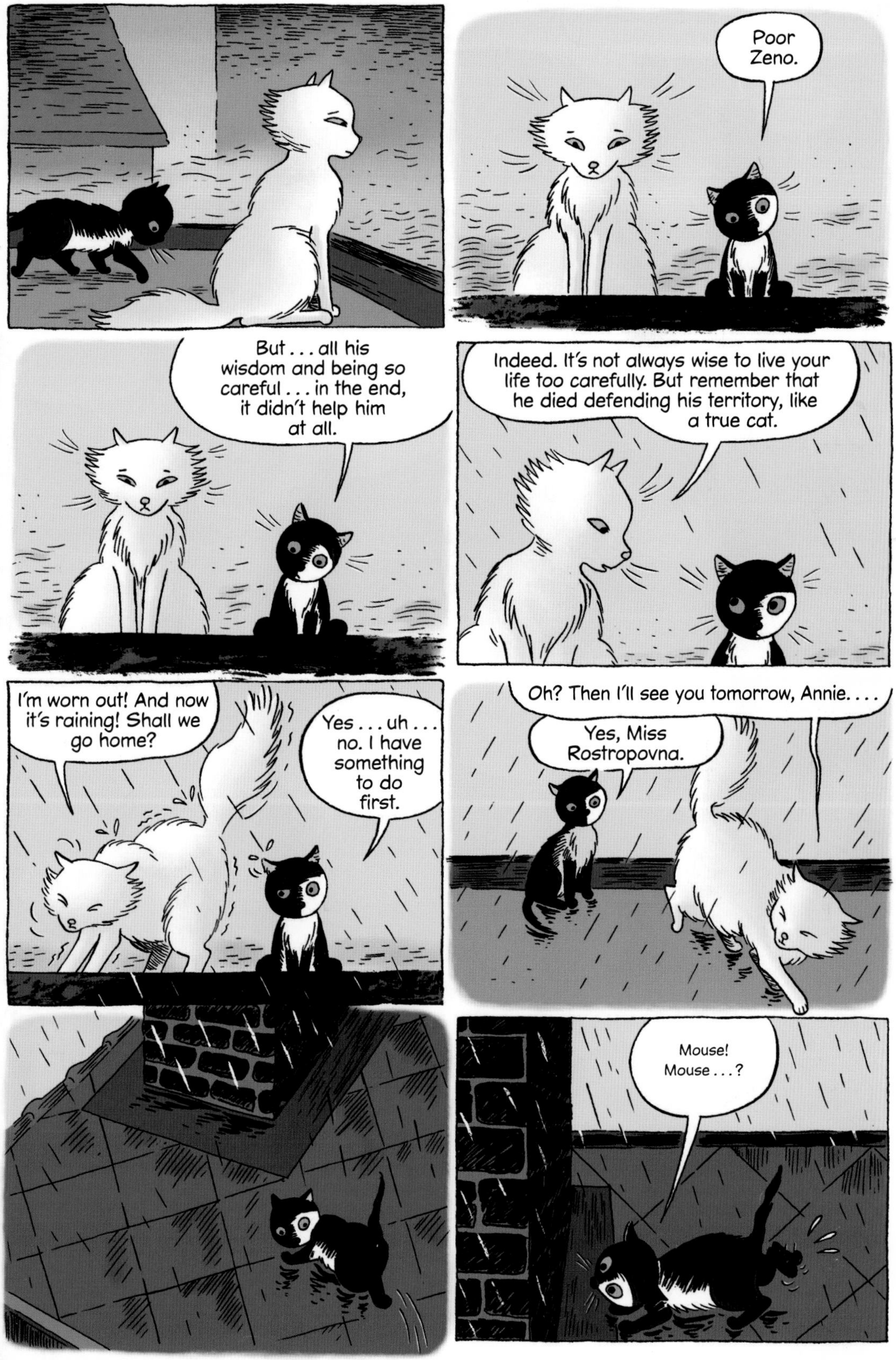
Poor Zeno.
But . . . all his wisdom and being so careful . . . in the end, it didn't help him at all.
Indeed. It's not always wise to live your life too carefully. But remember that he died defending his territory, like a true cat.
I'm worn out! And now it's raining! Shall we go home?
Yes . . . uh . . . no. I have something to do first.
Oh? Then I'll see you tomorrow, Annie. . . .
Yes, Miss Rostropovna.
Mouse! Mouse . . . ?

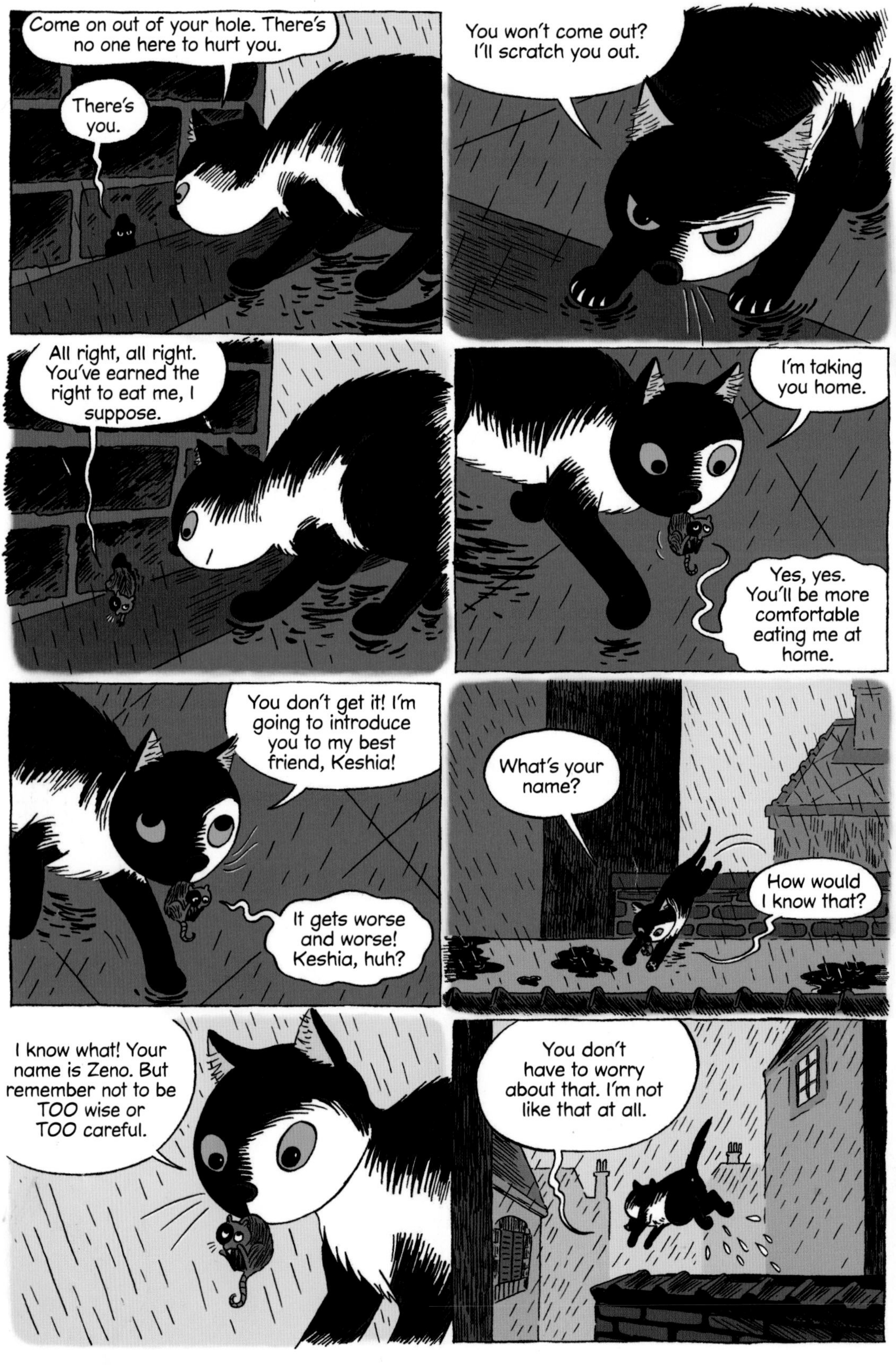
Come on out of your hole. There's no one here to hurt you.
There's you.
You won't come out? I'll scratch you out.
All right, all right. You've earned the right to eat me, I suppose.
I'm taking you home.
Yes, yes. You'll be more comfortable eating me at home.
You don't get it! I'm going to introduce you to my best friend, Keshia!
It gets worse and worse! Keshia, huh?
What's your name?
How would I know that?
I know what! Your name is Zeno. But remember not to be TOO wise or TOO careful.
You don't have to worry about that. I'm not like that at all.

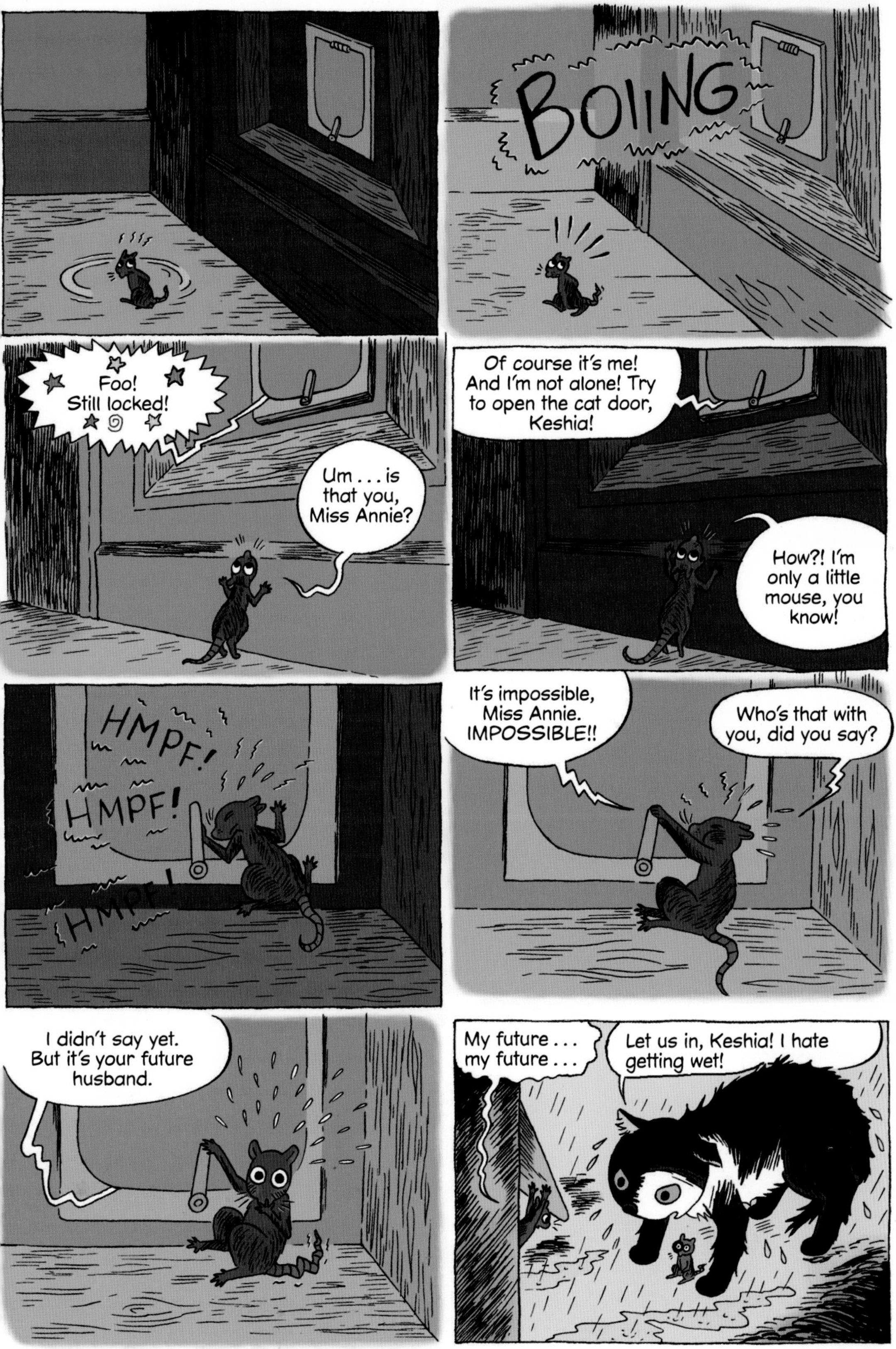
BOIING
Foo! Still locked!
Um . . . is that you, Miss Annie?
Of course it's me! And I'm not alone! Try to open the cat door, Keshia!
How?! I'm only a little mouse, you know!
HMPF!
HMPF!
HMPF!
It's impossible, Miss Annie. IMPOSSIBLE!!
Who's that with you, did you say?
I didn't say yet. But it's your future husband.
My future . . . my future . . .
Let us in, Keshia! I hate getting wet!

# Epilogue

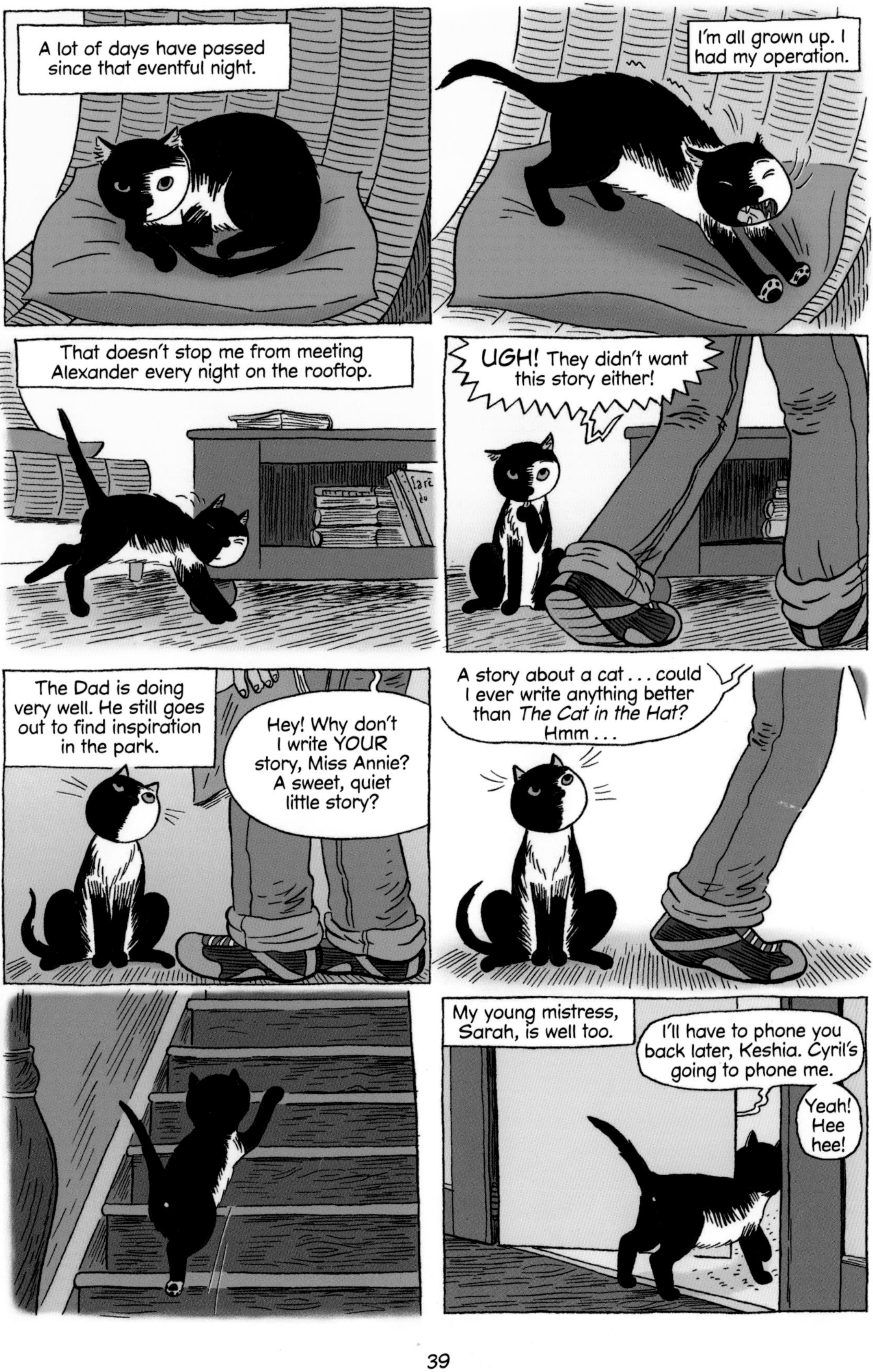
A lot of days have passed since that eventful night.
I'm all grown up. I had my operation.
That doesn't stop me from meeting Alexander every night on the rooftop.
UGH! They didn't want this story either!
The Dad is doing very well. He still goes out to find inspiration in the park.
Hey! Why don't I write YOUR story, Miss Annie? A sweet, quiet little story?
A story about a cat . . . could I ever write anything better than The Cat in the Hat? Hmm . . .
My young mistress, Sarah, is well too.
I'll have to phone you back later, Keshia. Cyril's going to phone me.
Yeah! Hee hee!

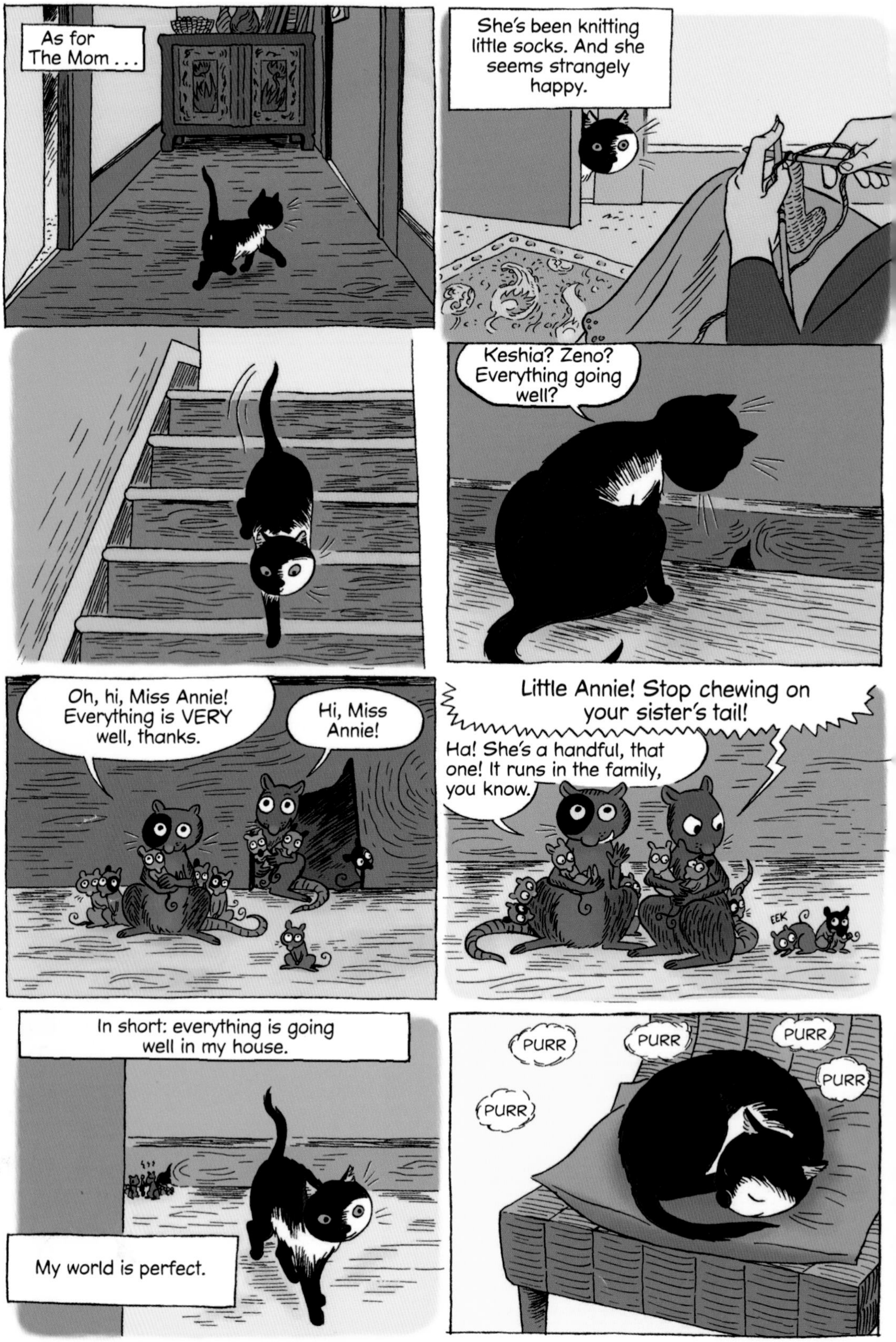
As for The Mom . . .
She's been knitting little socks. And she seems strangely happy.
Keshia? Zeno? Everything going well?
Oh, hi, Miss Annie! Everything is VERY well, thanks.
Hi, Miss Annie!
Little Annie! Stop chewing on your sister's tail!
Ha! She's a handful, that one! It runs in the family, you know.
EEK
In short: everything is going well in my house.
My world is perfect.
PURR
PURR
PURR
PURR
PURR

The End